GW00857475

This is a work of fiction. Names, characters, places, and incidents either are the product of the author's imagination or are used fictitiously. Any resemblance to actual persons, living or dead, events or locales is entirely coincidental.

First edition: May 2022

Illustrations copyright © 2022 by Priscilla Bampoh
Book cover and design by David Bushay
Edited by Elanor Best

ISBN: 978-1-8382576-2-0

www.leahosakwebooks.com

NONNY'S PUPPY LOVE:

BUST-UPS & BOY DRAMA

1

A lot can change in a week.

Your dad can *finally* forgive you for nearly turning his house into a food-splattered warzone at your DISASTROUS thirteenth birthday party.

Your evil arch-enemies can relentlessly heckle you as you walk through the school corridor, viciously yank your braids when nobody's looking, and spitefully threaten you and your best friends every chance they get – JUST when you thought they couldn't make your life any more hellish.

And… you can fall in love.

That's right. I'm in *love!*

All the TV shows I watch way past my bedtime have confirmed it. I always have so much in common with the girl who falls head over heels for the boy of her dreams. And no, I'm NOT crazy – it just makes sense. I've even written a list about it!

- ☑ She admires her crush from afar, WAY too afraid to speak to him.
- ☑ She scribbles her initials beside his over and over again, connecting them with hearts and flowers and other lovey-dovey doodles.
- ☑ She gets all tongue-tied and wobbly-kneed, even when he's on the completely OTHER SIDE of the room as her.

- ☑ She stares at her bedroom ceiling before she falls asleep, imagining them watching a movie at the cinema, then accidentally reaching for the popcorn at the EXACT same time so that their HANDS TOUCH!!

See? I *must* be in love!

Remember how Daniel and I had our first ever, PROPER conversation after my birthday? Well, that conversation was the start of something beautiful. And when I say beautiful, I mean… we actually *wave* at each other now. It's kind of our *thing*. And when he sees me in the school corridor, he'll look *right* at me, and with a hair-raising grin, say, "What's up, Nonny?",
EVEN when he's with all his super cool friends! *And* he asks to copy my Maths homework! Sometimes I'll hand it over before he can even utter the words.

Every time I walk into the Maths classroom and see Daniel at his desk, my lovesick heart bangs against my ribcage so loudly I'm sure the whole class can hear it, even though I pretend to be totally cool and chilled out. He sits right by the classroom door, so he's *always* the first person I see when I enter. I somehow, accidentally, kind of catch his eye and smile at him. It's not the big, show-all-teeth type of grin that I *really* want to give (I've got to play it cool, remember?), but every *single* time, he looks straight into my eyes, smiles back and... WAVES at me! Then, he'll say something *amazing* like, "You okay, Nonny?" or "Hey, Nonny!" Without fail, the butterflies in my stomach flitter and flutter like they've just broken out of their cocoons. Of course, I'll wave back and say, "I'm good, thanks!" or

"Hey, Daniel!" as calmly as my nerves will let me. Then, I float all the way to my desk at the back of the classroom, feeling FANTASTIC.

If he didn't like me, he wouldn't go the extra mile and actually *talk* to me. He would just smile, right? Not that him *just* smiling is a bad thing. Even with his teeth hiding behind those chunky silver braces, he still has the most heart-stopping smile ever. *Aahhhh!*

Sometimes I don't even know why I bother, though. There's NO WAY my parents would let me have a boyfriend. I know I'm thirteen and all, but I can't push my luck. I already tried asking my mum a couple of days ago.

"Mum… am I allowed to have a boyfriend?"

She snorted and raised her eyebrows at me. "What kind of boyfriend?"

I rolled my eyes. "You know… a *boy*friend."

"You can have a friend who's a boy, yes."

And that was the end of that. When I told my besties, they laughed hysterically.

"*My* mum said I can have a boyfriend, as long as I don't let him distract me from my studies," Nyah shrugged.

"Yeah, my mum doesn't care," Georgia said.

If only they knew how lucky they are.

Georgia's parents aren't together, so she gets DOUBLE freedom. She could have *two* boyfriends if she wanted – one here and one where her dad lives. Georgia's mum would let her boyfriend hang out at their house for as long as he likes. She'd probably even treat him to all of Georgia's favourite food (cheeseburgers, ham and pineapple pizza, and chocolate-chip muffins!), so that he'd NEVER want to leave. *Sigh.* And I bet Nyah's parents would splash out on fun day trips for Nyah and *her* boyfriend. They'd drop them at the seaside, or the bowling alley in town, and give Nyah a purse full of money to buy LOADS of snacks.

So, yep, it's just ME who's stuck with no choice but to be boyfriend-less. Not just because my parents want me to be alone forever, but because there's no one in the WHOLE WORLD I want except for Daniel. And he *isn't* my boyfriend.

Yet.

Just think... only a few weeks ago, he didn't even know my name. Now he *says* my name when he greets me. And he waves at me every day, which means he'll *soon* be asking me to hang out after school (until my mum barks at me to come home at four o'clock, of course).

Georgia and Nyah know I have a crush on Daniel. Ever since our conversation after my party, he's ALL I can talk about. (Well, not *all*. But I definitely talk about him more than I ever have before.) Sometimes I don't even realise I'm doing it.

"Daniel asked me if he could copy my homework today."

"Daniel waved at me AGAIN today!"

"Daniel looks so nice today."

They roll their eyes, pretend to retch, and Georgia, as expected, tells me I'm acting like a lunatic.

"You're *crazy,* Nonny. You're acting like the stalker from that scary movie we watched at my house. I bet you watch him from outside his bedroom window every night! With binoculars!" she hoots.

I laugh along with her. Even *I* wouldn't go *that* far.

"I'm not *crazy,*" I insist. "He's just so *cool.* And he's really nice, too," I protest.

"Yeah, but you don't even *talk* to him. He probably thinks you're a crazy weirdo, just staring at him all the time and not saying anything! Like this." She sits stiff and upright like a statue and stares into the distance, her eyes as wide as saucers.

Nyah chuckles.

I can't help but laugh too, but that's *exactly*

why I won't tell them how *much* of a crush I have on him. That information is as sacred as my stones that comfort me when I'm feeling anxious. It's staying safe and locked away FOREVER. Well, until we're boyfriend and girlfriend, of course. And I think we're moving closer to that! Because today, on what I thought would be just an ordinary Wednesday morning, something *wonderful* happens.

As usual, I coast into the Maths classroom, pretending to be engrossed in my phone. (As we all know, that's *Nyah's* thing, not mine. The only time I'm on my phone is when I'm reading the only texts I ever get: the ones from my mum telling me to "COME HOME NOW!", or from my BFFs sharing silly videos and planning our next sleepover.) I notice Daniel out of the corner of my eye, unpacking his backpack. Just as I'm about to look up and smile at him, he gently taps my arm.

I freeze, even though my insides are on fire. Daniel just *touched* me. To get *my* attention! He's NEVER done that before! AAAAAHH! This must mean something, right? I think this means we're getting closer... right?

"Hey, Nonny!" he beams.

I gulp and jam my phone into my pocket before it slips from my sweaty hands and smashes into a billion shards by Daniel's feet. I face him, tingling with nerves.

"Hey, Daniel," I smile back, this time with my teeth.

"Have you done the homework?" he hisses, covering his mouth with his left hand so that Miss Hill doesn't see what he's saying.

I nod, as always, because this is pretty much our weekly routine. Even though he *knows* the answer (my dad won't allow me to do *anything* until all my homework is done), he'll still ask. And I'll always say yes because I could *never* say no to Daniel. I'll shuffle closer and reach into my bag (discreetly, of course) to retrieve my homework. He'll slither his hand across his desk, his eyeballs fixed firmly on Miss Hill, and snap the piece of paper up like a chameleon latching onto a fruit fly. We'll snigger like rebels, his braces will glimmer as he thanks me, and I'll head to my desk.

It's our inside joke – the equivalent of our own special, secret handshake.

We go through that same routine today.

"Thanks, Nonny," he whispers, stuffing my homework into his pocket, ready to copy it during the lesson.

"You're welcome," I grin.

"I can't wait until breaktime already," he says. "I'm *starving!*"

I nod wildly in agreement. To be honest, he could have said, "I love the smell of wet dog", and I *still* would have had the same reaction. I just LOVE speaking to him.

"Same!" I declare, even though I'm really not that hungry at all. "I really want a white chocolate chip cookie, like RIGHT now. They're the best," I sigh for dramatic effect. I'm so proud of myself for not tripping over my words.

"Oh *man,* they're my favourite!" he exclaims, his mouth stretching into a warm smile. "I would have them for breakfast, lunch AND dinner if I could!"

I snicker hysterically. Daniel is SO funny.

"Okay, class! Seats, please!" Miss Hill yaps, interrupting our beautiful moment.

I'm sad our chat has to end so abruptly, but I'm ecstatic we said more than five words to each other! As I practically dance all the way to my desk, I can feel the light imprint of his hand on my blazer sleeve. *Aaahhh!* I *never* want to wash it again.

...Okay, maybe I *am* a little bit crazy, like Georgia said. But don't worry, there's no WAY

I could get away with not washing my school uniform. My mum would *kill* me.

I collapse into my seat, barely able to concentrate. I replay what just happened in my head, while the love of my life copies my homework.

After what feels like hours of watching Daniel scribble away, breaktime finally comes. Loud, hungry students rush over to Miss Hill to hand in their homework, antsy to grab the best cookies from the canteen. I hang back, then sneakily scuttle over to Daniel. His braces make a welcome appearance as I approach him.

"Thanks again, Nonny. I don't know how you do it; you're just so clever!" he gushes. "I owe you one."

Oh. My. Gosh.

Daniel just said I'm CLEVER! And that he *owes* me one! EEEEK! I giggle girlishly as he passes the wrinkled piece of paper back to me (I kind of wish he wouldn't shove it in his pocket so clumsily, but *obviously* I'd never tell him that. *Especially* now that he just said he thinks I'm clever!). As he adds his freshly copied homework to the growing pile on Miss Hill's desk, I hurriedly smooth out the creases in mine.

He turns back to me as I finish, a cheeky grin on his face. "See you later then, Nonny."

"Bye, Daniel," I squeak, my cheeks flushing.

Aaahhh, I just wish I could say something else! Something cool, or funny, or *interesting.* Something that'll make him *really* like me. I gaze at him as he leaves the classroom and ambles down the corridor, his backpack slung lazily over one shoulder. I sigh, totally lovestruck. Then, I neatly place my homework on top of his.

Feeling on top of the world, I hurry to meet Georgia and Nyah. I barge through the noisy crowds in the canteen, accidentally squishing a couple of stray grapes under my shoe. Georgia's sitting alone, devouring a packet of salt and vinegar crisps.

"Hey, Georgia," I grin as I plonk myself opposite her, putting my bag down on the table.

Georgia inspects my face suspiciously. "Why are you so *happy*? Wait… don't say anything. You just had Maths? And that means you just spent the whole time staring at *Daniel*, and wishing you were *married* to him and–"

"Shut *up*, Georgia!" I cry, rolling my eyes.

Her voice can be seriously loud sometimes, and I don't want Daniel walking past and thinking I'm *insane*.

Half of me wants to tell her about the moment we just had, so that I can share my happiness with someone else, but the other half of me *knows* that she'll laugh in my face and tell me I'm bonkers, *yet again*.

While I'm still contemplating whether to tell her the good news, Georgia starts chuckling.

"What?" I ask, giggling along with her.

Every time Georgia laughs, it makes *me* laugh, even *before* she's told me the joke. It's so contagious – it brews all the way down in her belly, rumbles in her throat, and erupts from her mouth like lava.

"Daniel was *so* funny in Spanish this morning."

My laugh stops just as fast as my heart. *WHAT?*

"He meant to say that he likes eating eggs, right? But instead – oh my gosh, Nonny, it was *soooo* funny – he said, he said..."

I wince as Georgia slaps the table with her hand, laughing so much that she can't finish her sentence.

She gasps for air while I reel in shock. Since when did she talk about *Daniel?* Since when did she find him *funny?*

My chest feels as tight as the ponytail on my head, but I try not to show it. I CAN'T let her know that simply finding my crush (who I've liked since the VERY FIRST DAY of Year Seven!!!) funny has made me feel this jealous.

"What did he say?" I smile weakly, wanting to get this pain over and done with as quickly as possible.

"He said… he said… he said he likes eating his SHOULDER!" Georgia shrieks, wiping a tear from the corner of her eye. "It was so funny, Nonny. Everyone was laughing so much. Even Mrs Blackwell was! And he was so embarrassed…"

I zone out as she babbles on and on about how funny Daniel is and how embarrassed he was. I don't get it – why does she find him SO hysterical all of a sudden? She never has before! I can feel my gaze drifting far into the distance, so I quickly shake my head to tune back into what she's saying.

"...Usually he doesn't say anything, so that's

why it was so funny. It's something *I'd* do, not him!"

I inhale sharply, prickling with irritation. Why does she think *she* knows Daniel all of a sudden? Only I know him. Okay, well, I don't *know* him, know him, but she doesn't know him AT ALL!

I chortle half-heartedly, when all I really want to do is burst into tears.

"That sounds funny," I croak.

Georgia nods excitedly. "It really was. You would have laughed so much, Nonny!"

I smile and clear my *very* dry throat. "Where's Nyah, anyway?" I ask, swiftly changing the subject.

I can't BEAR to talk about this for a moment longer.

Georgia takes a bite of a crisp. "Probably taking selfies in the toilet," she shrugs.

"Yeah, being a *wannabe*, as always," a

frightfully familiar voice quips.

Our heads snap up to see Amber Wartsworth strolling up to our table. Ugh. Becky Ritchcraft is so close behind her she's practically clipping her heels. They sneer at us. Georgia and I glare back.

"Who asked *you?*" Georgia glowers.

"And who asked *you* to keep eating all that junk food? Shouldn't you be trying to lose weight or doing some exercise or something?" Amber smirks.

"HA! She *definitely* should,"
Becky snipes.

Georgia sinks in her seat.

"Oh, just go *away,*" I growl.

Amber is the worst girl in the WORLD. And Becky is a close second. After I attacked Amber at my party (CRINGE!) they've stepped up the hatred for me and my best friends. Everywhere we turn, The Witches are there, waiting to pounce. Part of me doesn't blame them, since it was my fault for lunging at Amber and scratching her (annoyingly perfect) face.

"Shut up, Nonny. No one was talking to you."

"Don't say that Amber – she'll start *crying!*" Becky butts in while she can, her lip gloss shimmering like a disco ball.

"True," Amber snickers. "Nonny's such a *baby*."

I grit my teeth, my heart pounding with anger. I don't say a word. Maybe that way, they'll soon get bored and move on. Besides, I have more important things to worry about right now. Like the fact that my *best friend* suddenly finds Daniel extremely funny.

"Nonny's a baby, Georgia's a fatty, and Nyah's a weirdo wannabe," Amber sings, while Becky howls with laughter.

My eyes sting with the threat of tears but I dig my nails into my knees to stop myself from bawling. I won't let them see me cry EVER again. Georgia looks down into her packet of crisps, tight-lipped. When Georgia is silent, you know something is wrong. Even though I am slightly annoyed with her, I never want her to be upset.

The Witches strut away to ruin someone else's day, but the echo of their harsh laughter rings in my ears. Georgia frowns as she scrunches up the packet of crisps with one hand and pushes it away.

"I hate them so much," she mumbles.

"Don't listen to them, Georgia!" I cry. "They have nothing better to do than run around school being mean to everyone. You know everything they say is rubbish, right?"

Although it's the truth, I know I'm trying to convince myself just as much as her.

"I just don't know why they have to be so nasty."

"They're horrible people, that's all. But at least we have each other."

"Yeah. Thanks for sticking up for me, Nonny."

"That's okay, Georgia. You always stick up for me, too." I look around. "Where is Nyah anyway?"

"Who knows? But look, there's Daniel!" she grins.

My head jolts up at the sound of his name. But as I turn to look at him, a scorching sense of dread blazes through me.

Why does she sound so *excited?*

Daniel makes eye contact with both me AND Georgia, and gives us a cheerful wave. My hand is as heavy as lead when I lift it to wave back. Georgia is flapping hers with so much enthusiasm it looks like it might fall off!

I frown at her, my eyes narrowed and my brow furrowed. Waving at each other is *our* thing. Mine and Daniel's. Now *Georgia* is waving at him, too?

What is going on? Does she... *like* him?

A large lump swells in my throat. It's almost as big as the ones I find floating in the school custard at lunchtime. I need to calm down before my heart explodes. Just because he waved at us and she waved back like a crazy lady, baring all of her teeth, doesn't mean ANYTHING. If anything, it just confirms how friendly Daniel is.

"There she is! About time!" Georgia cries, beckoning Nyah over.

Nyah's braids swish from side to side as she walks over to join us. She huffs loudly as she finally sits down.

"Where have you *been?*" I prod.

Her fingertips tap-dance across her phone

screen as she types a message, ignoring my question. Georgia and I sigh loudly.

"See, I told you she was taking selfies, Nonny. She's probably posting one right now."

Georgia reaches back into her packet of crisps, then throws one at Nyah's head. It hits her right between the eyebrows.

"HEY! Why would you do that?" Nyah shrieks, chucking it back at Georgia who ducks just in time.

"Because Nonny asked you where you've been and you didn't answer, as always. Nyah! Earth to Nyah! Oh my goodness; can't you get off your phone for ONE second?"

"Can't you just wait?" Nyah yelps, locking her phone and pushing it into her blazer pocket. "I was taking a book back to the library, that's all."

Nyah's frown soon relaxes and she leans in close, as though she's about to tell us a secret.

Georgia and I glance at each other and shuffle forward until our foreheads are practically touching. Nyah always has good gossip, and I can just tell this is going to be EXTRA juicy.

"Guys," she starts, peering around to make sure no one is listening. She moves in closer and lowers her voice. "I like someone."

I gasp loudly. Georgia stamps her feet wildly. This is SO exciting! Boys always like Nyah (how could they not? She's fashionable, pretty, and has dimples and amazing braids), but she NEVER likes them back.

"Who, who, who? Oh my gosh, let me guess! I bet it's Josh Harries!" Georgia squeals.

"Shhh, Georgia! Let Nyah tell us! Since *when,* Nyah?"

Nyah laughs nervously, shifting restlessly in her seat. "Since today."

"Today?!" Georgia and I squawk simultaneously.

Nyah nods. "I only just spoke to him properly. He's so nice," she sighs.

"Who is it? Tell us now!" I shriek, pulling on her arm.

"He's over there," she murmurs, pointing ahead.

My eyes follow her finger. I see Iesha, then I see Daniel, then Cleo and Chioma. I whip my head back to her, confused. Am I looking in the right place for her mystery crush?

"Where–" I start.

But before I can finish my sentence, it hits me like a painful jab in the stomach. I turn back to the crowd of people, my head spinning and my heart throbbing.

He looks up, catches my eye, and waves. But this time, I can't wave back.

It's Daniel.

She likes Daniel.

2

"You like DANIEL?" Georgia shrieks.

"Yeah," Nyah shrugs coolly, as though this is the most normal thing in the world. "What's wrong with that? Nonny likes him too!"

Nyah looks at me for approval, but all I can muster is a faint nod before my eyes travel to a splodge of dried ketchup on the table.

"Well... s-so do I," Georgia admits coyly, her cheeks reddening.

I stare at her, horrified. I KNEW IT! But I

can't say a thing because my jaw is glued shut. All I can do is blink back tears. First Nyah, now Georgia? And on the same day? My heart feels like it's being buried by a barrel of thick, gloopy cement. It's sinking so fast I feel dizzy.

How did this happen?

"I guess we all like him, then," Nyah shrugs.

Why is she so cool about this? Am I the only one who cares?!

"Nonny was right; he's actually really cool. And he's funny," Georgia grins. "But wait… isn't it a bit weird that we *all* like him?"

Yes. *Yes.* YES!

"No. Why would it be weird? It's not like any of us are gonna be his girlfriend!" Nyah declares, popping a grape into her mouth.

I flinch.

"I'M going to be his girlfriend!!!" I wish I could scream. But nothing comes out, not even a peep. I need some water – NOW.

"True. I don't even want a boyfriend, anyway. Oh my gosh, this is so funny – we all like the same boy!" Georgia giggles.

"I know, right? I was just in the library and I bumped into him by accident. It was like something out of a movie!" Nyah breathes, playing with one of her braids. "Then he said sorry and he – he… *winked* at me! Then we started talking–"

I stand abruptly, scraping the chair across the floor with such force that my besties stop in their tracks to gawk at me.

"Erm… I have to go… I forgot I-I… See you later," I stutter, my voice wobbling.

I grab my bag before they can question me and race all the way to the toilet, gnawing at my bottom lip to hold in the tears.

As soon as I lock the cubicle door behind me, the waterworks burst free. This can't be happening. Just this morning, everything was going SO well! Daniel and I were getting closer. He *touched* my arm! So, who would have thought that my two BEST FRIENDS would be the ones to bulldoze their way into our budding romance?!

I tear off endless sheets of toilet paper, wipe my tears, and blow my nose as I sit down. The whole time I was wondering where my best friend was, she was in the library, flirting and laughing and winking with MY crush! Why did Daniel have to wink at Nyah, anyway? He's never winked at *me* before! Or did she make it up to try and make me jealous? Hmmm, yeah… maybe she made it up. Daniel doesn't wink.

But… what if he does?

Thoughts race through my head like they're competing on Sports Day. The bell rings, but I can't leave just yet. I've got English with Georgia now, and I can't think of anything worse than sitting next to her and pretending that everything is okay. Not when she has a CRUSH on the LOVE of my life! Plus, my eyes are all puffy and sore, anyway.

I blow my nose again and flop against the wall, defeated.

How am I going to stand out against Georgia and Nyah? Georgia, with her crazy laugh and fun nature, could win Daniel over any day. Daniel could take one look at Nyah and fall in love with her modelesque looks, her heaps of confidence and her expensive clothes.

Then there's me. There's nothing particularly special about me. I'm not popular on social media like Nyah, or charming and outgoing like Georgia. I'm as quiet as a mouse, I play with stones like a five-year-old and all I do is cry – according to The Witches. They're right anyway, because more tears stream down my face as I think about this morning's events. Daniel would *never* choose me over my besties!

So *what* if I let him copy my homework every week? Georgia can woo him with her captivating personality and Nyah can amaze him with her fancy house and cool style.

"This is so unfair," I whisper to myself.

The end-of-break-time racket brings me back to my senses. Boys are chanting and hooting like hooligans at a football match. Teachers are yelling at everyone to "STOP RUNNING NOW!" and hundreds of shoes squeak across the polished floorboards.

Stop crying, Nonny. Everything will be fine. Plus, you don't want to prove The Witches right!

I wipe my tears with the now-sodden tissue and flush it down the toilet. I think back to my birthday party. If that disaster taught me anything, it's that I NEED my friends. And that no matter how I feel right now, everything will get better.

So, it's time to face Georgia.

She's already sitting in her seat when I arrive. She beams at me as I sit down, and I suddenly feel bad for being mad at her.

"Where did you go?" she asks.

Ahhh! I haven't had time to think of a lie yet because I've been so busy snivelling and feeling sorry for myself.

Think, Nonny, think.

"Oh, I, uh, just went to the toilet," I stammer, holding my breath.

It is the truth, after all.

"Oh, cool," she says. "I really can't be bothered with this lesson. I wish we were outside sunbathing right now! Look how sunny it is!"

Phew. She doesn't suspect anything. Now I can just pretend that nothing ever happened.

"I know, right. We should sunbathe at lunch," I say.

"Yeah, let's!" she grins.

I start to slip into my daily Daniel daydream while Mrs Sandhu blabs on about how important it is to use quotes in our essays. But a light nudge from Georgia brings me back to reality.

"Nonny, guess what?" she hisses.

Mrs Sandhu clears her throat, glaring at Georgia beadily. "Would you like to share that with the rest of the class, Georgia?" she calls.

Everybody turns to look at us, sniggering.

"No, miss," Georgia mumbles.

"Right, I didn't think so. No talking when I'm talking, please."

"Sorry, miss."

Mrs Sandhu nods and carries on. Out of the corner of my eye, I see Georgia rip a piece of paper from her workbook and start scrawling. Georgia and I always pass notes to each other in English. Even her whisper is loud, so this is the safest way to communicate and avoid detention. She slides the note across the table and underneath my hand. I silently, carefully move it to my lap to read it.

I wish I didn't.

Guess what!!! Daniel asked me if we could be partners for our Spanish presentation next week!!

NO, NO, NO!

So many questions whir through my head while my heart is being crushed like a can of cola.

When did he ask you this?!

Why am I crazy when I talk about him but YOU'RE not?!

Why are you taking him away from me?!?!

I can sense Georgia eagerly awaiting my reply, so I inhale deeply and weakly pick up my pen.

Did u say yes?

of course!! He's sooo good at spanish so I have to make sure I practise loads!! otherwise I will embarresass myself!

Haha when did he ask u?

After u went to the toilet at break

Noooo! It's all my fault! If I hadn't stormed off in a tizzy, Daniel would NEVER have asked Georgia to be his partner! Or… did he wait *until* I was gone to ask her?! But… *why* would he do that?

I quickly hide the note as Mrs Sandhu cruises past our desk. I usually hate it when she interrupts our secret conversations, but today, I'm glad she does. It's a good excuse for me to crumple the piece of paper up and 'forget to reply'.

The rest of the lesson is a blur. Questions and worries swim around my mind as I desperately try not to cry. I nervously tap my pen against the table until Sophia Simmons shoots daggers at me. Oops.

I can't let this get me down.

No. No WAY! I just have to step it up, that's all. I don't know *how,* exactly. But I have to! If Daniel is busy bumping into Nyah in the library and asking Georgia to be his Spanish partner, I *need* to do something extraordinary! That way, he won't just be asking to copy my boring, old *Maths* homework. He'll be ringing me after school and asking me to hang out at the weekend (when he eventually asks for my number)!

I just have to figure out what to do.

By the time I get home, I'm EXHAUSTED from the emotional rollercoaster I've had to ride today. I yell "Hi, mum! Hi, Isaac!" as I leap up the stairs, then dive headfirst into bed. I bury my face in my pillow and let out a muffled scream. What do I do *now?* Do I finally admit my real feelings for Daniel to my BFFs? Do I tell them that I *love* him so that they can back off? No, I can't. It's too late. They'll just think I'm doing it because I'm jealous.

Frustration churns through my bones. *This* is what happens when you keep secrets. ARGH – if only I had told Georgia and Nyah how I really felt right from the start, then none of this would have happened! There are SO many other boys at school they could like. There's Josh Harries, who has piercing blue eyes and a mischievous smile. He causes a lot of trouble, but he gets away with *everything* because everyone loves him, even the teachers. Or there's Fred Williams, who has floppy blonde hair and dazzling white teeth. He makes all the girls swoon because he's a professional swimmer outside of school and has *muscles.*

So, why *Daniel?*

I hug my pillow to my chest and rack my brains, thinking up clever ways I can get Daniel to notice me properly.

Hmmm… I could tell him some jokes I found on the internet to make him laugh? *No way. That could backfire terribly; he might not find me funny at all!*

How about I buy him an ice cream from the canteen at lunchtime tomorrow? *What am I thinking – I don't even have enough pocket money to scrape together for myself, let alone Daniel too.*

I could share my sweets with him during Maths? Offer to copy my own homework for him, so he doesn't have to?

Just as I'm about to give up hope… DING! A wonderful idea pops into my head.

I sit up in bed and grin widely. I've got it! I know *exactly* what I'm going to do.

Things are about to change – starting from tomorrow.

3

BEEP, BEEP, BEEP, BEE–

"Uggghhh!" I groan, as I switch off the alarm on my phone with a swipe of my finger.

I rub my eyes, stretch and slowly swing my legs out of bed. It's half past six. I'm NEVER up this early, but today is a *special* day. It's Get Daniel To Notice Me Properly Day.

I tiptoe across the landing and slink into the bathroom to shower. I feel like a thief in the night, but I struggle getting out of bed at half seven on a normal day, so I don't want any suspicious questions from my parents this morning.

Once I'm dressed and ready to go, I gather all the equipment I need and dump it into my school bag. It's time to put my plan into action.

I get to school even earlier than the caretaker. The corridors are practically empty; it's almost spooky. I scurry to the toilet, park myself in front of one of the only mirrors that isn't cracked, and start unpacking everything I need. I pull out my mascara, my cherry-flavoured lip gloss and the small pot of foundation I swiped from the back of my mum's bathroom cabinet. She'll never realise it's missing.

There's no way I could do my makeup at home. If my dad had caught me this morning, I'd be getting home-schooled for the rest of the *week!* Don't ask me why it's such a big deal. I already tried to put up a fight a few months ago.

"Why am I not allowed to wear makeup? Everyone else is!" I wailed.

"Are you everyone else?" my dad blasted.

"Georgia's and Nyah's parents let them wear makeup! It's not fair!"

"While you're under *my* roof, you'll do as I say. Go and live with your friends if you can't stick to the rules!"

Sometimes I *really* wish I could. I'd be able to wear as much makeup as I want, stay up as late as I want and DO whatever I want. But I could never leave my poor little brother, Isaac, at home with the Professional Party Poopers.

"It's not a fashion show, Nonny. It's school. And you're too young to be wearing makeup, anyway. Your friends shouldn't be wearing it either," my mum chimed in.

"Do you *want* people to think I'm weird? I'm probably the only girl in school who doesn't wear it – and it's because of YOU guys!" I scowled.

"Stop backchatting and go and tidy your room now. NOW!"

Now do you see why I had to wake up at the crack of dawn and trek all the way to school to do my makeup?

Anyway, it'll be worth it. I've got Maths for first period, so Daniel is going to be SO delighted when he sees me! I make sure I do my mascara just as flawlessly as Nyah does hers: it's never clumpy, and *never* ends up on her eyelids. And when Georgia applies her foundation, she blends it in like an *expert*, so I try my hardest to follow in her footsteps too.

I've done a great job, if I do say so myself! I mean, if my super long lashes, shimmery lips and glowing skin don't get Daniel's attention, I don't know what will.

I slide my pink clips into my braids, pack my things back up and head to the potted plants to meet my friends. Nyah's already there, leaning against the wall and scrolling through her phone.

"Hey, Nyah!" I chirp, approaching her.

She does a double-take, her mouth flying open in awe.

"Oh my gosh, Nonny! I almost didn't recognise you! You look AMAZING!" she cries.

"Thanks!" I smile broadly.

"You *never* wear makeup! Did your parents let you wear it today?"

I hesitate. "Well… they didn't see me. I-I snuck out before they could," I fib.

Well, it's *almost* true. I *did* sneak out – just not as fearlessly as Nyah thinks.

"Wow, you're brave," she chuckles. "How comes you decided to wear it today, anyway?"

"Just felt like it, I guess," I shrug.

I'm lying through my teeth, but she doesn't need to know that. No one needs to know that I've covered my face in makeup to impress Daniel.

Georgia soon joins us, but not before she grinds to a halt and ogles me from head to toe.

"Nonny! You look *beautiful!* Why are you wearing makeup today? Did your mum finally say you could?" she gasps.

I laugh and shake my head, ready to tell yet *another* white lie. "Nope. I just felt like wearing it today."

"Well, I think you should be allowed to wear it *every* day. You should just tell your parents that you're a teenager now, and that's what teenagers do!"

"I wish it was that easy," I sigh.

"Well, I think you look fantastic," Georgia says. "*Sooo...* can I borrow your lip gloss, please?"

"Thanks, Georgia. Sure," I say, rummaging around in my bag to find it.

I hand it over as the bell rings.

"Yay! Thanks, Nonny. Oh my gosh, it smells amazing. Nyah… Nyah? Smell this!"

I'm already halfway down the corridor while Georgia struggles to get Nyah's attention, as if speed-walking to my form room will help time go faster.

"See you at break, guys!" I call over my shoulder.

I can't sit still at ALL during form time.

"'Ave ya got ants in ya pants or somefin'?" Billy Fletcher guffaws, nudging his posse of friends and pointing at me. "Guys, look. Nonny's got ants in 'er pants!"

I roll my eyes as they all splutter with laughter. The only attention I need right now is from Daniel, not Silly Billy and his annoying gang. *Aaah,* I can't WAIT to see the shock on Daniel's face when he looks up, waves, and gets a load of my new, glamorous appearance. Eeeek!

As soon as the bell rings, I launch out of my seat and aim for the door faster than Mr Greaves can say "Have a good day, Year Eight!"

I slow down as I reach the Maths classroom. I'm *never* this early, so I don't want to look *too* keen. I smooth my braids into place, rub my lips together to spread the gloss, and wipe my increasingly moist palms on my skirt.

In I go.

I look down at the floor when I enter (trying to play it cool, as always), then slowly lift my gaze to make eye contact with… Daniel's empty seat.

I frown.

Where is he? He's usually unpacking the contents of his rucksack when I enter the room. But today, I find myself staring at his bare desk like I've seen a ghost.

I exhale loudly. *Great.*

"Everything okay, Nonny?" Miss Hill asks, studying me closely through her long, brown fringe.

"Yes, miss," I mumble, dragging myself to my seat.

Ugh – my plan has *already* backfired. Daniel was supposed to see me first thing this morning, be so mesmerised that he can't focus for the rest of the day and forget ALL about chasing after Georgia and Nyah!

It's fine. He'll show up. He *always* comes to Maths; he's just late, that's all.

But twenty minutes pass, and he's still not here.

Tick-tock, tick-tock.

I stare at the clock so hard my eyes start to water. Thirty minutes go by.

Give up, Nonny. He's not coming.

Just my luck. It happened at my party, and

it's happening again now. I sag into my seat, feeling like a real class clown – minus the funny jokes – with this stupid makeup painted on my face.

If you thought I didn't listen in Maths before, I'm *certainly* not listening now. Who cares about trigonometry, anyway?

Sadly, I realise that Georgia has Spanish next period, which means that Daniel does too. I squeeze my eyes shut, hoping and wishing and praying that he doesn't show up to *that* lesson either.

As I dawdle through the corridor to get to my next lesson, Joe from History catches up with me.

"You look really nice today, Nonny," he smiles.

"Thanks, Joe," I beam back, secretly blushing underneath countless layers of my mum's foundation.

"So… does your dad still hate me?" he chortles.

Ugh – I wish he would forget about the fact that my dad chased him out of my birthday party with my mum's slipper.

Cringe.

"*No,*" I sigh. "I'm sorry about that, by the way."

Joe shrugs. "It's okay. I found it funny. But your dad is *scary!*"

"You're telling *me!*" I say.

We get to the classroom and I sit down at my desk, feeling conflicted. Even though it feels AMAZING to get a compliment, I know that it would feel ten times *more* amazing if it had come from Daniel. My shoulders droop mournfully. What's the point of wearing all this makeup if Daniel's not even here to see it? I just want to scrub my face clean.

I've never felt more relieved when the bell finally rings. I can't wait to see my BFFs at breaktime and distract myself from my terribly failed plan.

I take a seat next to Nyah, who's got her phone in one hand and a bunch of grapes in the other. Georgia's munching on a questionable-looking sandwich from the canteen.

"Hey, guys," I say, dropping my bag by my feet and narrowly missing a puddle of spilt milk.

Breaktime is always chaos. Either The Witches are flying around on their broomsticks, torturing their latest victim, or there's ear-splitting noise hitting me from every angle. I look around the canteen, imagining how peaceful it would be if–

DANIEL?!

Daniel's here?!

I sit up straight and brush invisible dust off my blazer in a frenzy.

"Daniel's here?" I squeak, to no one in particular.

"Oh yeah, I just had Spanish with him. He said he felt sick this morning so he tried to stay at home but his mum *forced* him to come in! Poor him," Georgia reveals.

"Poor Daniel," Nyah agrees.

"Oh," I murmur, willing the love of my life to at least glance in my direction.

Hello... hello... over here!

"And you'll *never* guess what, guys!" Georgia presses on.

I swallow, sensing bad news. My temperature is rising already. I don't want to guess. I don't want to *know*.

"What? Tell us!" Nyah squeals.

"Well... I was sitting next to Daniel, right?"

Keep it together, Nonny.

I nibble on one of Nyah's grapes to stay composed.

"Riiight..." Nyah urges, impatiently waiting for Georgia's bombshell.

"And basically, yeah, he said he liked my lip gloss – thanks Nonny – and then he came *soooo* close to my face to smell it. I really thought he was going to KISS me!" she shrieks.

I nearly choke on my grape, which has suddenly turned into tasteless mush in my mouth.

"No way!" Nyah cries, clapping her hands excitedly. "Nonny, did you hear that?" she giggles.

I nod, wearing a strained smile, and force the soggy grape down my throat.

So, let me get this straight. Daniel said he liked Georgia's lip gloss, which is actually *MY* lip gloss, so he leant towards her and nearly KISSED her, which he would have done to ME if he'd have come to MATHS! I want to scream. Georgia couldn't have known that was going to happen when she borrowed my lip gloss, but I'm still so *mad* at her! Did she even tell Daniel that it was *mine?* I'm trembling with rage. Daniel should have been leaning in close to my face and nearly kissing *me* – not Georgia!

"Well, he winked at me again today," Nyah boasts, using her phone as a mirror to check out her hair.

"He winks at everyone," Georgia retorts flatly.

SINCE WHEN???

"No, he doesn't. You're only saying that

because he winked at me yesterday, too."

"No, I'm not. It's true. I saw him winking at Kemi earlier. He doesn't just wink at *you*."

"I've never seen him wink at anyone before, Georgia. You're just jealous that he winked at me and not you."

"Me?" Georgia screeches. *"You're* just jealous that we nearly kissed today!"

Nyah snorts with laughter, a little too loudly. "As *if!* Anyway, it's not like you actually *did* kiss."

I sit in silence, my mouth feeling like it's been rammed with cotton wool. Georgia and Nyah are getting winks, near kisses, and secret proposals to be Daniel's partner for Spanish presentations. But all I get is a measly *wave* and a couple of short-lived conversations every now and then?!

I can't let this happen anymore. Something needs to change before Daniel ends up forgetting about me completely. I HAVE to up my game – and fast. For the first time in my life, I might have to *compete* with my best friends.

And all I can say is… may the best girl win.

"NONNY!" my mum blares across the landing. "WHERE'S MY FOUNDATION?"

Whoops! I scramble out of bed in a haze and frantically empty my school bag onto the carpet to find it. I didn't think she'd realise I'd taken it! I patter into the bathroom, nervous to face my angry mum.

"Sorry, mum," I murmur sheepishly, handing it to her.

She hurls me a dirty look as she snatches it back. "What have I told you about going through my things? And don't make me tell your dad that you've been wearing makeup. You know you're not supposed to!"

"I said I'm *sorry,*" I whine.

I don't even *want* her silly foundation anymore, anyway. After Daniel missed Maths last Thursday, I was so deflated that I didn't bother wearing it again. He probably wouldn't even have noticed it, what with he and Georgia nearly sharing a smooch that same day. *Sigh.*

"Don't go through my things again, Nonny. I mean it!" my mum snarls, stabbing her index finger at me.

Nyah *always* goes through *her* mum's things and she NEVER gets told off! But then again, Nyah gets everything she wants – *including* winks from Daniel.

"And what are you doing? Why aren't you ready for school?"

"I'm getting ready *now*," I lie, rubbing my eyes.

I literally just woke up, which means I'm going to be late.

"Go and get dressed. Right now."

I swivel and stomp to my room, grumbling under my breath. I don't WANT to go to school today. It's Monday, and that means it's the day of Georgia's Spanish presentation with Daniel. It's the only thing I'm going to hear about ALL DAY and I just cannot bear it.

But I'm wrong, because at breaktime, I'm hit with *another* blow. This time, from Nyah.

"Guys, I think I'm gonna ask Daniel to come round my house," she announces, drumming out a rhythm on the table with her polished nails.

Ughhhh! I just KNEW that today was going to be a bad day.

"You don't even know him," I say, trying my best to stop my voice from quivering.

"I *do,* actually. We bump into each other all the time now," Nyah grins, showing off her gorgeous dimples. "Plus, he asked me to return his books to the library for him on Friday. I said yes, and then he said he *owes* me one."

Wait, *what?*

That's what he said to *me!* I didn't realise he'd started asking my *friends* for favours too.

Ugh. I wish I was as bold and confident as my friends. Nyah has NO problems asking Daniel to hang out at her house, while I can't even pluck up the courage to speak to him about anything other than Maths. How boring.

"Doesn't mean you *know* him," Georgia chips in, agreeing with me. "But whatever. I bet he'll *love* your house!"

Nyah's house is very cool. It's full of vivid colours and wacky furniture (Nyah even has a hot-pink wardrobe!) and I just know that Daniel will LOVE it. He'll probably love it so much that he'll start doing his *own* Maths homework from the comfort of her room and never want to copy mine AGAIN!

Nyah's eyes twinkle. "I'm gonna ask him when I see him today! Eeeek, I can't wait!"

Nyah doesn't even have to ask her parents first; she knows they'll say yes. It's so unfair. No matter how hard I beg or how many chores I do, my parents would NEVER let me invite a member of the male species round to our house. Even if he's as sweet as Daniel.

Ugh – he'll be so impressed by Nyah's lavish lifestyle that he'll forget I ever existed. There's no way he can EVER go to her house.

I mosey into the Maths classroom with my eyes locked on my phone. Daniel's already at his desk, organising his pencil case.

"Hey, Nonny!" he calls.

"Oh, hey, Daniel. I didn't see you there," I giggle, acting startled.

He chuckles. "You okay?"

Come on, Nonny. Keep this conversation going.

"Yeah, I'm fine, thanks!" I chirp. "You?"

"Yeah, I'm okay. It's kinda boring sitting here, though. You should ask Miss Hill if you can sit at the front with me!"

I stare at him, awestruck. My heartbeat speeds up, slows down, then stops altogether. Did he just say what I *think* he said? Did he just say that he wants to sit next to *me?!*

"Oh, erm, yeah, haha, I t-totally should. I–I mean I'd love to," I bumble awkwardly.

Heat rises from the soles of my feet to the top of my head, setting my face ablaze. *That was terrible, Nonny. You can do better!*

"It'd be *much* easier for you to copy my homework that way," I continue, praying that he'll laugh at my desperate attempt at a joke.

And he does! YESSS! I cool down a little.

"Exactly!" he titters. "*And* you could share my snacks with me! I brought *loads* in today."

Daniel wants to share his snacks with *me?* He's so sweet!

"You have snacks?" I gasp.

Everyone smuggles snacks into their lessons, so I'm not shocked at all. I just really don't want this conversation to end.

"Yep," he replies, looking pleased with himself. "Look."

He beckons me closer with a small wave of his hand, then opens his backpack to reveal a secret stash of gummy sweets, a packet of cheesy puffs and a nutty chocolate bar. I step into his space, feeling sparks fly, shoot and soar between us. I'm so close to him that if I take one more step, our fingertips will DEFINITELY touch.

Wow. So, *this* is what it feels like to be close to Daniel. Scents of warm vanilla and freshly washed bedsheets fill my nose. *Aaahhh* – how I *wish* I'd worn my lip gloss today!

My lip gloss.

I come crashing back down to earth, a frown on my face. Georgia and Daniel. *Nyah* and Daniel. *Ugh*.

"Amazing!" I breathe, suddenly discouraged.

"I know, right?" he smirks, zipping his backpack shut and placing it on the floor. "Anyway, you must be pretty popular. You're *always* on your phone."

I must look confused, because he points to the phone that is, in fact, sitting in my hand. My eyes follow his finger, and I immediately want to laugh. He has no idea that it's all for show, that I only pretend to constantly be on my phone so I can appear cool as I walk past him. I'm about to fiercely deny my popularity – but then something clicks in my mind, like a light finally switching on after hours of darkness.

Should I…?

I take a deep breath. Here goes.

"Yeah… I'm getting like my best friend, Nyah," I laugh. "She's *always* on her phone."

Daniel's face lights up, much to my despair. "Oh, I know Nyah!"

I know you do.

"Do you?" I ask sweetly.

Daniel nods. "Yeah, she's really nice."

I know she is.

"Yeah, she is." I pause, ready to make my next move. *Nyah's your best friend, Nonny. Are you really going to do this?* "Her parents aren't that nice, though," I whisper, screwing up my nose.

Ugh, I did it.

I suddenly feel *horrible*. I LOVE Nyah's parents, and they love me. They're the coolest, most stylish parents I've ever known. But I'm desperate to make sure Daniel *doesn't* go to Nyah's house. If he does, I'll well and truly lose him forever.

Daniel's eyes stretch in shock. "Really? What do you mean?"

I swallow. "Well… they're always… yelling. Every time I go round her house, they're arguing about something. It's… it's quite scary sometimes."

I notice Daniel's expression changing from shock to horror. He's buying it!

"And – and she'd kill me if she knew I'd told anyone this, so you probably shouldn't say anything, but Nyah's dad *hates* it when she brings people over. *Especially* boys," I lie. "He might even be worse than *my* dad!" I add for good measure.

That'll *really* put him off.

This might be the biggest lie I've EVER told. Nyah's parents are welcoming, friendly and *super* laidback. I've made them sound like the worst people on earth, but there's no going back now.

Sorry Nyah's mum, sorry Nyah's dad!

"Oh man, that sounds bad! I'm never going to *her* house, then!" he sniggers. "And don't worry, I won't say anything."

I laugh with him, feeling flustered. Phew. Even though my stomach is tied up in knots because I've what I've just done to my best friend, I *am* pretty pleased. Daniel's definitely not going to Nyah's house, and we just had *another* proper conversation – hopefully one of many! Mission accomplished!

But when I see Nyah storming towards me and Georgia at lunch, all I want to do is scoop her up in a big hug and tell her how sorry I am for badmouthing her amazing parents. She looks furious. I quickly try to push my guilt to the back of my mind before she sits down.

"You'll never guess what, guys," Nyah huffs.

"What?" I ask innocently, although I'm pretty sure what she's about to say.

"So, I just saw Daniel. I asked him if he wanted to come round. And he said *no*," she exclaims, looking confused.

I hold my breath.

Georgia gasps, horrified. "Why did he say no? That's so rude of him!" she cries.

Nyah shrugs. "I have no idea. I was *sure* he was going to say yes!"

"What exactly did he say?" Georgia asks.

"All he said was that he couldn't come and that he was sorry. He didn't even ask to reschedule," Nyah scowls.

I'd better say something quickly, before they get suspicious.

"Oh dear," I add.

That was pathetic, Nonny.

"Yeah… weird, right? Anyway, whatever. That's the last time I'm inviting *him* to my house. *And* the last time I'm taking his stupid books back to the library for him. He was probably just using me anyway. I'm over it," she sniffs, flicking her braids off her shoulder.

Well… that was easier than I thought.

I'm in the clear – I *think*. Nyah doesn't seem too upset, so that makes me feel better for being so awfully sneaky. Inside, I'm spinning, cartwheeling and screaming "WOOHOO!!!" but I don't give my happiness away. Plus, I have worse things to worry about now. Georgia's been fretting about her presentation *all* day, just like I thought she would.

"I've been practising all weekend, but I *still* don't know it off by heart yet! I'm gonna have to read my notes in front of the whole class, which is gonna be so embarrassing," she sulks.

"Oh, stop worrying, Georgia," Nyah sighs, putting her phone on the table. "You'll be *fine*. You're just stressing yourself out for no reason. My mum says that when you're nervous, you should take ten deep breaths," she declares.

"I can't do that right now," Georgia moans. "Daniel is counting on me to get this right. He asked if I could write his lines for him because he didn't have time. So, I wrote his first, and he said he's memorised them already! But I took so long writing *his* that I didn't have enough time to write or memorise *mine!* I need to practise NOW, or he'll *kill* me."

I secretly roll my eyes. *Daniel, Daniel, Daniel.* And she once called ME crazy! I tune out as Georgia practises her Spanish lines, holding her cue cards in front of her like a news reporter. I *wish* I could go back to being my normal self so I could comfort my best friend and wish her luck, but I just can't bring myself to right now.

I'm still upset with her for getting so close to Daniel and nearly kissing him with MY lip gloss on!

"Ahh, guys, I feel sick. I'm gonna go to the toilet. Can you look after my bag please, Nonny?" Georgia spouts, jumping up from the table and gripping her stomach.

"Sure," I nod.

Usually, I'd feel terrible seeing my bestie in such a state, but I can't help but feel annoyed. She's only this nervous because she's trying to impress *Daniel*. She even prepared the whole presentation, just for him!

Georgia tucks her notes back into her bag and dashes off, looking queasy. Nyah is tittering away at something on her phone. That's good – she already seems to have gotten over Daniel declining her invitation earlier. Nyah's tough; she won't let a silly rejection from Daniel bring her down. The guilt tied tightly around my neck slowly loosens.

I chew on my stale chicken and sweetcorn baguette, reluctantly waiting for Georgia to return from her emergency trip to the toilet. It's then that I catch a glimpse of her cue cards. They're peeking out the corner of her bag, just… *staring* at me.

What if I just…? No.

No.

But… if Georgia just *lost* her notes, then…

NO.

I shake my head, trying to remove the dreadful thought that just wriggled its way in. I could never do such a thing. Georgia's my best friend; I would *never* do that to her.

But my hands act before my brain does. I whip the cue cards out of Georgia's bag like a Pickpocketing Pro and push them deep into my bag, my heart thumping ferociously. I peer up to see if I've been caught, but Nyah is still wrapped up in her online world to notice my betrayal.

Phew.

My forehead is damp, so I dab it quickly before Georgia gets back to the table. I don't even have time to think about what I've done.

"Are you okay, Nonny? You look like you're about to pass out," Georgia frowns, as she sits back down next to me.

I bob my head up and down as normally as I can, crazily wringing my hands underneath the table. *Act cool, Nonny. Act cool!*

"Yeah, I'm fine."

"Are you sure? You can have some of my juice if you like."

Don't be nice to me, Georgia. I'm a terrible, terrible person. I shake my head and manage a watery smile.

"If you say so. Gosh, I'm so nervous. What if I completely mess up and embarrass myself in front of everyone?" Georgia gulps.

"You won't, don't worry," I croak.

I glance at my best friend, her beautiful brown curls pulled back into a ponytail and her plump cheeks flushed with nerves. I feel like the worst person in the world – even worse than The Witches. I desperately want to push the cue cards back into her bag and forget this ever happened. This isn't me. I don't want to do this to my best friend.

"You'll be fine, Georgia. It's not like it's your GCSE exam," Nyah says.

"I *know*, but Daniel is so good at Spanish. And he asked *me* of all people to be his partner, so I don't want to let him down. Plus, he's been so nice to me and I would feel terrible if I messed this up. Oooh, Nonny, please can I borrow your lip gloss again, actually?"

I take it back.

I can't listen to her bang on about Daniel ANY longer. I *have* to do this.

"I don't have it, sorry," I say.

"Oh man. That's okay."

The bell rings and we all stand, gathering up our things for afternoon form time.

"Well," Georgia breathes. "This is it, guys. Wish me luck!" she squeals, crossing both her middle fingers over her index fingers and shaking her hands in the air.

"Good luck, Georgia!" Nyah sings.

"Good luck!" I echo.

This is it.

***

I've been anxious all evening. I can't even play with Isaac and his beloved train set. I just need to know what happened with Georgia and Daniel. I *need* to know if what I did at lunchtime means she and Daniel will finally stop talking.

By the time I get a text, I've nearly pulled out all my eyelashes and eaten an entire bag of chocolate biscuits (I'm going to get in a *lot* of trouble when my parents find out). It's Georgia. She's sent a message to our group chat.

Georgia: Hey guys, are u free for a phone call? x

Nyah: Yeah sure :)

Me: Yeah I am x

Eeeek! It's the moment of truth. I watch my phone closely, anticipating the second Georgia's name flashes across the screen. I tap 'Answer' before I even hear the ringtone.

"Georgia?" I ask, plodding over to the window and looking outside onto the street. A blue car speeds down the road.

A dishevelled cat scurries into a bush.

"N-nonny, I-I-I'm so upset," she snivels, gasping for air.

Oh no.

Oh *no.* I didn't think she'd CRY!

"Georgia? Are you *crying?*" Nyah asks, worried.

"It was horrible, guys. It was *horrible.*"

I gulp and walk back over to my bed. I sit on the edge, suddenly very nervous.

"W-what happened, Georgia?" I utter.

"You know how scared I was to do this presentation, right? Well, right before Spanish, I was just starting to calm down and – and… oh gosh, it's *awful,*" she cries, blowing her nose loudly. "Daniel came up to me and he was *so* kind and lovely and nice. He said, "We've got this, Georgia", and I felt so ready to get up in front of the class and do it. But then… but then…" she wails.

"*What,* Georgia? Please stop crying! I hate hearing you cry!" Nyah exclaims.

"I couldn't find my notes ANYWHERE! But I only realised *right* before it was our turn! Guys, I was *sooo* scared. I was shaking and everything! I tried SO hard to remember everything I had written but it just wouldn't come to me," she blubs. "It was the most embarrassing moment of my entire LIFE!"

The sound of her crying is gut-wrenching. "Oh, Georgia, I'm so sorry," I mumble, feeling like a monster.

"Oh no! I feel so sorry for you, Georgia. You worked so hard," Nyah soothes.

I start to pace around the room. Do I tell her that I took her notes? Do I put an end to this right now? No, I can't; she'll HATE me!

"I just don't know where I put my notes! I had them with you guys at lunch, and then POOF! They just disappeared into thin air. I don't *get* it," Georgia sobs. "But that's not even the worst part."

"What happened?" Nyah asks.

"Daniel hates me. Guys, he *hates* me!"

"I'm sure he doesn't, Georgia. It's not your fault–"

"It IS my fault, Nyah, because I lost my notes! I should've just learnt them off by heart like a normal person. Like Daniel! You should have seen the way he looked at me, guys. He was so angry with me. And what makes it even worse is that I *wrote* the whole thing, so I should have been the one to memorise it! Ugh – I'm so *stupid*."

"No, you're not! He'll get over it, Georgia. It's – it's just a silly presentation," I stammer, now perching on the edge of my desk, which suddenly feels like the edge of a cliff.

But I know he won't get over it. Because this is what I wanted to happen – I steal Georgia's notes, Daniel gets mad at her, then he turns his attention back on me. I just didn't realise it would be this bad.

"He won't get over it. He said he couldn't *believe* I didn't know my part. Now Mrs Blackwell will give us lower marks... and it's all because of ME!" she howls.

An ice-cold shower of guilt washes over me. I shiver.

"Oh, Georgia," Nyah sniffs. "I can't believe that happened. So, Daniel's really mad at you, then?"

"He's so mad at me, Nyah. He said he's not gonna work with me again because he felt so embarrassed. Ahhh, I just feel so stupid!"

"Look on the bright side, Georgia. At least he doesn't just hate *you*. He hates both of us now!" Nyah giggles. "Plus, he didn't even do any of the work himself! You did it all for him, so he shouldn't get any credit, anyway!"

"I guess," Georgia snuffles.

My plan worked. I should feel triumphant! I should be bouncing off the walls. But I sit stock-still, as if I've turned into the stones I hide under my bed. I got what I wanted; Daniel is *finally* backing off and staying away from my friends. So why do I feel so rotten?

We all say our goodbyes, Georgia still whimpering at the end of the phone. I'm lost for words, something heavy and painful clamping down on my chest. I walk over to my bed, crouch down beside it and pull my box of stones towards me. Breathing deeply and slowly, I clutch my Magic Stone – my favourite, most precious one – and try to calm down. It's cool to the touch. I roll it between my palms, its smoothness a *much* better sensation than the clammy sweat I felt while Georgia was crying. Even though it's a dark shade of grey, it's not dull, or miserable. In fact, it's the opposite. My eyes follow the white line that runs around the middle of it until I feel dizzy. After a few minutes, I *do* feel slightly better, but I still feel terribly guilty. I gently return my Magic Stone to its home and drag myself to my feet.

With my head in my hands, I flop onto my bed and start to cry.

What have I done?

5

My eyes are red-raw on Tuesday morning, and my whole body feels like I've run a marathon for TEN hours straight! Getting out of bed is even harder than usual.

I brush my teeth lazily, feeling super anxious. How on *earth* am I going to face my besties today? Ugh – I can't *bear* to see Georgia's tear-streaked face or hear about how annoyed Nyah is with Daniel for rejecting her invitation. I know I'm being a silly little scaredy-cat, but it's ALL my fault and I feel so guilty.

I walk the long way to school, hacking my way through scraggly weeds and wandering down winding roads like an explorer. My mum says I should NEVER come this way because I'll get kidnapped – but this is an emergency! I need to get to school late so I can steer well clear of my BFFs. One peek at my face and they'll just *know* something's up. I've also decided I'm going to spend breaktime AND lunchtime hiding away in the library, burying my head in a book that I definitely won't want to read. I have English with Georgia later today, but I can *easily* hide in the toilet instead. I feel atrocious, running away from my best friend when she's so upset, but this is the way it needs to be – at least until everything goes back to normal and she forgets that Daniel ever existed.

Sigh; who knows when I'll *ever* be able to spend time with my besties again?

***

"How are you feeling now, Georgia?" Nyah asks at breaktime.

Okay, so, I couldn't avoid them forever. I *tried* to skulk to the library once the bell went after Science, but Nyah spotted me, linked my arm and dragged me to the canteen, where Georgia was already waiting. I've barely said a word.

Georgia exhales. "I feel okay. I told my mum about it last night and she made me feel so much better. She told me something like that had happened to her when *she* was at school. She was in a play and she..." Georgia's voice fades out and she crouches down in her seat, trying to hide. "Daniel just walked in," she whispers.

Nyah and I look up to see the boy of my *(our)* dreams sauntering towards us.

"Don't *look!*" Georgia hisses, shielding her

face with one hand, as though that'll make her invisible.

Daniel walks past to greet his friends and Georgia finally relaxes.

"Ugh, I do NOT want to go to Spanish today. I'm gonna have to change seats. He won't want to sit next to me anymore," Georgia whines.

My stomach clenches. I no longer have the appetite for my iced donut. I *hate* that I've made her this worried.

"Don't worry, Georgia. He's not worth it," Nyah says. "So *what* if he didn't want to come to my house and he doesn't want to sit next to you anymore? It's his loss. That's what my mum says."

Nyah told *her* mum too? Her kind, trendy, *cool* mum who I told vicious lies about? Great! I'm not listening to their conversation anymore. I wish I *had* gone to the library after all. I can't think straight; my brain is filled with shame.

But even though I feel loathsome, I can't help but stare longingly at Daniel as my BFFs natter about how awful he is. It's not true – he's *not* awful. He's funny, he's kind-hearted and… I *guess* he's all mine again. Right? Despite upsetting my bestest friends in the whole wide world, my plan to stop them from taking Daniel away from me *worked*. This is what I wanted all along! I've got to enjoy this moment, otherwise humiliating Georgia and deceiving Nyah would have all been for NOTHING.

And now that I've got Daniel all to myself again, I feel *much* more confident when I walk into Maths the next day. I wear my cherry-flavoured lip gloss again, hoping that he'll notice and lean in close to *me* this time.

"Hi, Daniel!" I say cheerily, grinning at him.

He looks up from his school planner and smiles at me, his brown eyes sparkling.

"Hey, Nonny," he replies, doing a double take. "Your lips look… shiny."

I gasp silently. OH MY GOSH. He noticed!

"Yeah," I giggle, stepping a little closer to his desk. "I'm wearing lip gloss today!"

"Oh, cool! I swear every girl wears that stuff."

That's not the point, Daniel!

"Uh… I guess. This one is cherry-flavoured," I continue, hoping with all my might that he'll ask to smell it.

"Oh, yeah! Georgia was wearing that the other day, wasn't she? Smells good! By the way, have you done the homework?"

I roll my eyes internally, but my smile stays plastered to my face. Of *course* he wouldn't ask to smell it; he already HAS, because GEORGIA wore it FIRST!

"Yep," I mutter through gritted teeth, getting my homework out of my bag and handing it over. "Here you go."

"Cheers, Nonny. You're the best," he beams,

keeping his eyes on Miss Hill while he tucks my homework into his school planner.

I hover by his desk like an irritating fly, waiting for him to say something more. To look at me again. But he doesn't. Embarrassed and disgruntled, I make my way to my desk. I thought things would be different today. I thought that now he doesn't speak to Georgia and Nyah anymore, he would pay more attention to *me!* But everything is the same – if not WORSE! I'm not even sure my plan was worth it, so now I just feel like an even more lousy friend.

"Nonny? Are you here with us?" Miss Hill smirks, rudely barging in on my thoughts.

I sit up straight, flustered. "Uh… sorry, Miss. W-what did you say?" I mumble.

She scoffs while the rest of the class look at me and giggle, Daniel included. *Ugh.*

"Can someone *please* tell Nonny what we're

talking about?" she sneers, brushing her fringe from her eyes with her hand.

Chioma raises her arm.

"Go for it, Chioma."

"We're talking about integers," Chioma says proudly. "Which number on the board is an integer?"

I don't CARE about integers right now!!!

"Errrrm…" I hesitate, trapped by all these eyes on me. "Err… sixty-seven thousand?"

Miss Hill raises her eyebrows. "Hmmm, well done. Eyes on the board, everyone!"

Phew.

I can breathe again. Once everyone has had a good laugh at my expense and turned back to the board, I fan myself with my hand to cool down from the embarrassment. I glare at the back of Daniel's head, mad at him for laughing at me and mad at him for not noticing me properly! In my daydreams, we're eating lunch together, hanging out after school and texting every evening by now. In reality, all he does is copy my measly homework. What's the point?

For the next couple of days, I'm the Bestest Friend You Could Ever Imagine. Even though Georgia and Nyah know nothing about what I've done, I *need* to make it up to them. So, I let Georgia borrow my lip gloss whenever she asks (what use is it to me now, anyway?), and I take all the pictures of Nyah that she wants, not moaning even ONCE!

Daniel *still* waves at me and says, "What's up, Nonny?" whenever he sees me, and I *still* go weak at the knees and can barely breathe. But that's as far as it goes. *Humph.*

By Friday, my best friends seem to have totally forgotten about Daniel. They don't talk about him anymore, and Georgia doesn't hide away when he walks past our table in the canteen. I'm relieved; this means that I won't have to go on any more secret missions to scare Daniel off, which means I NEVER have to do anything like this to my besties again. *Phew.*

Friday lunchtime is always the best, and today is even better. This weird week of feeling like an evil person is finally coming to an end, *and* it's the only day that we get to eat CHIPS at school! Plus, Friday lunchtimes are usually when my besties and I plan our next sleepover, which we're doing right now.

"I know what we should do tomorrow!" Nyah says, her mouth full of pizza. "We should do our makeup and hair, *then* we should make up a dance routine! And we can post it online, too! I've seen so many people do it recently."

Georgia pretends to vomit. "Bleurgh! No way. That is so embarrassing!"

"Humph! What's *your* idea then?"

"*I* think we should ride our bikes into town, then go around the shops. Yeah, ask your mums for some money so we can go shopping!" Georgia suggests, her eyes widening with excitement. "Then, we can go to the park, get chicken and chips, then go back to my house and watch movies."

"Why do you always have to have everything *your* way? What if I don't want to go on a boring, old bike ride?" Nyah snaps.

"Well, it's a much better idea than *dancing*. I hate dancing!"

"You hate everything! What do *you* want to do, Nonny?"

You know what I hate? Being in the middle. If I choose Nyah's idea, then Georgia will be mad at me. If I choose Georgia's idea, then *Nyah* will be mad at me. I can't win!

"Erm… how about–"

"Wait. What do you mean I hate everything?" Georgia butts in, frowning. "Just because I don't like everything you like doesn't mean I hate everything!"

"You never want to do the things I suggest. You only want to do everything *you* say and that's not fair."

"That is SUCH a lie! If we always do everything I want to do, then how come you and Nonny never complain about it?" Georgia bites back, her face reddening.

I can tell she's getting very angry.

I take a deep breath. I don't want to get involved in their argument. "Guys, can you just stop, please?"

They don't even look at me.

"Because you always like to argue!" Nyah exclaims. "You can't keep being so bossy. It's not fair."

"Stop telling me what to do. You're not my mum!" Georgia blasts. She sticks her fingers in her ears and shuts her eyes to block out Nyah's lecture. "Lalalala," she sings.

"You're only doing that because you know what I'm saying is *true!*" Nyah continues, raising her voice over Georgia's out-of-tune melody.

"Lalalala, leave me alone."

"Stop being so BOSSY, then maybe I will!"

"I *said*… leave. Me. Alone," Georgia snarls, opening her eyes and removing her fingers from her ears.

"I'll leave you alone if you stop–"

"Leave me ALONE!" Georgia bellows, banging her fists on the table.

The quake causes her opened bottle of orange juice to splash all over Nyah's blouse and beautiful braids, right before it tumbles over and floods the table – *and* Nyah's phone.

"GEORGIA!!!" Nyah roars, jumping up and grabbing her most prized possession. She shakes it like a tambourine to remove the orange juice, then desperately wipes it on her skirt. Georgia stays put, her arms folded and a scowl on her face.

"My hair! And my *phone!*" Nyah cries.

Orange liquid drips from the ends of her braids like melting wax from a candle. She's *furious.* People are turning to stare and point at us. I'm so embarrassed by the scene my two best friends are causing.

"Nyah, sit down," I hiss. "Georgia didn't mean to do that. Did you, Georgia?" I say, grabbing Nyah's arm to stop her from rushing off. Georgia doesn't say a word.

"Let *go,* Nonny! I need to go and get some tissues to clean my phone. It's probably broken because of *her!*" Nyah yaps, thrusting her index finger in Georgia's direction.

"Just *wait,* Nyah. I have tissues. Sit down, *please!*" I beg.

Nyah gives Georgia a dirty look and reluctantly sits down. I sigh with relief. I hate it when my besties argue. I already feel bad enough about going behind their backs with all my Daniel shenanigans, so I don't want *them* to be squabbling too.

I tip my bag to the side, trying to find these tissues FAST, before Nyah gets impatient and storms off without making up with Georgia. My hand scrambles around in the darkness, feeling forgotten hair bands and old chocolate bars that I haven't eaten. *Ah* – there they are! A few things fall out of my bag as I pull the packet of tissues out like a rabbit from a hat.

"Thanks," Nonny grunts, taking a few.

Georgia gathers my things for me while I help a grumbling Nyah dry her juice-soaked blouse and braids.

"Thanks, Georgia," I smile, as she puts my school planner and a few stray pens back into my bag.

It can be so tiring when Georgia and Nyah argue. They're both extremely stubborn, and I'm *way* too scared to take sides, so–

Wait.

No.

No, no, no.

There's a cue card on the table.

But it's not my cue card. And that's not *my* handwriting. It's Georgia's.

IT'S GEORGIA'S!!!

My temperature soars. I HAVE to get to Georgia's Spanish notes before she does! I HAVE to get to them NOW and wedge them back into the depths of my bag before–

"Isn't this mine?" Georgia asks, grabbing the cue card with a quizzical look on her face.

Gulp. Too late.

I say nothing, my gut plummeting to my feet like I'm on a crazy ride at the theme park. I couldn't say anything even if I wanted to; my tongue is suddenly stapled to the roof of my mouth.

"Why do you have…?" Georgia starts, before her eyes widen and she slowly lifts her head to look at me. It's the same look my dad gives me when I'm still in bed on a Saturday morning instead of doing my chores.

I can't look at her. I'm being suffocated by my collar and my shirt is clinging to my back. I've been caught red-handed.

"It was *YOU?*" Georgia shrieks, her face turning crimson. "*YOU* took my Spanish notes?"

Nyah stops drying her hair and gapes at me. *"What?"*

I squirm in my seat as two sets of bewildered eyes bore into me. My armpits are drenched.

"I… uh…" I slur, feeling woozy.

Georgia's hands shake with anger as she grips the card that I stole from her. Silence hangs in the air like a putrid smell, until Nyah starts giggling. She stops when we both turn to stare at her.

"What? It's just… Nonny wouldn't do that!"

"Shut up, Nyah. What do *you* know?" Georgia flares.

I push my plate of lasagne and chips away, trying to think about what I can say to excuse my dreadful behaviour. I could say that it was an accident, that I must have put her notes in my bag without thinking. Or I could say that I was keeping them safe for her when she went to the toilet, but just forgot to give them back. But… I can't.

"Sorry," I whisper. I clear my throat and try again. "I'm sorry," I say, louder this time.

And I really mean it. I look down at my

hands, which are quivering just as much as Georgia's.

"You're *sorry?* Why would you *do* this to me, Nonny? I don't understand. So, what… you just *took* my notes when I wasn't looking or something?"

"I-I don't know. I… yes," I mumble. Tears fill my eyes. "I'm so sorry, Georgia. I-I don't know what I was thinking."

"So, it's because of *you* that I embarrassed myself in front of EVERYONE, and it's because of *you* that *Daniel…*" Georgia trails off, her brow furrowed. She claps her hand to her mouth, shocked. "*Daniel.* You did this because of Daniel, didn't you?!" she shrieks.

I burst into tears, feeling so ashamed.

"I'm sorry, Georgia. I… I was just so *jealous.* But as soon as I knew you were upset, I felt so, so bad. And I wish I hadn't done it. It's because… well, it's because… I really wanted

Daniel to like just *me...*"

I shut up when I realise how silly I sound.

Nyah starts sniggering again. I glare at her. Now is NOT the time to be laughing.

"Sorry. It's just... I can't *believe* you would do something like that. It's so... *savage,*" she chuckles.

I know she's only laughing like this to get revenge on Georgia for showering her hair and phone in orange juice.

"I don't know why *you're* laughing, Nyah. How do you know that *Nonny* didn't have something to do with Daniel not coming to YOUR house?" Georgia spits.

I freeze.

This. Can't. Be. Happening.

Why won't the ground just turn into a huge black hole and gobble me up right now?

Nyah spins her head round so fast her braids nearly whip me in the face. She watches me, waiting for me to explain, but my mouth just opens and closes like a startled goldfish.

"Oh. My. Gosh. You *did,* didn't you?" Nyah gasps, her pupils piercing into me like knives.

I look down, saying nothing. But my silence says everything.

"What the *heck,* Nonny? Why on earth would you DO that?" she hollers.

"I… I really don't know. I'm so sorry," I blub. But I *do* know. I was jealous and selfish, and I didn't think of the consequences that my ghastly actions would have on my friends' feelings OR our friendship. I was only thinking of myself. "Guys, I'm so, so sorry. I just wanted Daniel to like *me*. I promise I'll NEVER do anything like this–"

"What did you say to him?" Nyah quizzes, cutting me off.

I gulp. "I-I can't remember," I blurt, before I can stop myself.

I *need* to stop lying, but I just can't bring myself to tell her what I said about her lovely parents.

"What did you *say*, Nonny?"

"Uh… erm…" I garble, panicking. "J-just that–"

"Spit it *out*, Nonny."

I wish she would leave it. I *really* don't want to reveal the full details of my betrayal.

"I… I… said something terrible," I mumble, my eyes closed. My knee will NOT stop shaking. "I said… your parents are always arguing and shouting and that… and that your dad hates boys being in the house."

"*Woooow*," Georgia exhales, shocked by my monstrous lies.

"I am so, so, SO sorry, Nyah!" I sob, opening my eyes to see both Georgia and Nyah goggling at me as if an imposter has just entered my body.

I don't blame them. I *feel* like a different person.

"You know what? I don't even want to hear your apology," Nyah spits.

"I can't believe you would do that to us, Nonny," Georgia rants. "And don't think we're going to forgive you just because you're *crying*. You weren't even going to say a word until all that stuff fell out your bag!"

I cover my face with my hands in shame. "I'm *sorry*."

"You're just sorry you got caught," Nyah snaps.

That feels like a stab to the chest.

She gets up to leave and Georgia follows, but I'm fused to the seat like there's extra-strong Velcro on my school skirt. I watch my besties walk away from me and our friendship, my vision clouded by tears. Maybe they're right. Maybe I *am* just sorry I got caught, because that's what happens when you're a horrible person. And that's who I am now: a horrible person. I wish I could turn back time. Not even my Magic Stone can fix this feeling.

I dart to what seems to be my new favourite place: the toilet cubicle. I feel safe here, even if the smell makes me want to throw up the two forkfuls of lukewarm lasagne I just forced down. Everything's RUINED! My best friends of all time now *hate* me, and they probably will FOREVER! Why did I have to let a boy get in the way of our once unbreakable bond?

Voices drift into the toilet, disturbing my much-needed time alone. I roll my eyes, annoyed.

"You coming round tonight, then?"

Ugh – I recognise that horrid, high-pitched voice. It's Amber. As if my day couldn't get any worse.

"Yeah, deffo," Becky replies.

I can just imagine her adjusting her push-up bra and re-applying her lip gloss in the mirror.

I'd better keep quiet. With their witchy senses, they'll probably be able to sniff out my scent like police dogs at a murder scene.

"So, did you talk to him today?" Amber asks.

Ooooh. My ears prick up and I lean a little closer to the cubicle door, trying to hear who The Witches are talking about. This could be exciting gossip to share with my best–

My heart sinks.

You don't have best friends anymore, remember?

I sit back, no longer interested in what my arch-enemies have to say.

"Yep," Becky answers, smug as can be. "He said he liked my hair."

"No *way*. He *definitely* likes you. Wait – Becky, don't *do* that with my blusher. You're using way too much!"

"Oh… sorry, Amber. Yeah, I think he likes me too. Can I use *this* much?"

"Hmmm, yeah that's fine. My mum says that if you put too much blusher on, you'll look like a clown. So, what are you gonna do, then?"

"Yeah… you're right. Well, I might ask him

to hang out after school next week. Should I?"

"*See!* That looks SO much better. Yeah, I totally think you should."

"Do you *really* think he likes me, Amber?"

"Of course he does. He said he liked your hair!"

"Yeah, true. I've never heard him say that to anyone else before. Thanks for letting me use your blusher."

"That's okay. No – no, close it *properly,* Becky. And yeah, he *deffo* doesn't say that to anyone else. Anyway, I think you'd make SUCH a cute couple."

"Thanks, Amber. Me too. All the losers will be so jealous," Becky boasts. "Just you watch – I'm *going* to make Daniel my boyfriend."

I should be packing my overnight bag for a sleepover with my besties today. But everything's different.

I wake up with knots in my stomach, feeling as anxious as the hour before my thirteenth birthday party. Maybe even *more*. I check my phone to see if I've been greeted by a text from Nyah, as she's normally up the earliest out of the three of us. (Usually, I'm praying for a message from Daniel, which would be a serious miracle because he *obviously* doesn't have my number.) But a blank screen stares back at me. I sigh and slam my phone down on the bed.

The only thing that can cheer me up right now is a HUGE plate of food. I tried cradling a handful of stones last night, but that did no good. Maybe I really *am* outgrowing them. So, now, all I can think about is stuffing my face with something delicious to make me feel better – preferably scrambled eggs on toast, sprinkled with cheese and drowning in ketchup. My mum usually makes it on a Saturday morning, and when I trudge into the kitchen, I'm delighted to see my plate already waiting for me. I embrace Isaac in a tight hug.

"Get off me, Nonny!" he squeals, shrieking with laughter.

"Get off him, Nonny," my mum says sternly.

As I sit down, I notice my pink and white bike outside the window, resting against the garden shed. I should have been going on a bike ride in the sun with my BFFs today. (Yep, I liked Georgia's idea the best. I wish I had just spoken up at the time. Then she and Nyah wouldn't have had that huge argument, and NONE of this would have happened.) I burst into tears.

My mum looks at me, aghast. "What's wrong, Nonny?"

"N-n-nothing," I whimper, stretching my sleeves over my hands and wiping my eyes.

"This is not nothing. Why are you crying?"

My mum puts the kettle on the side and places her arm around my shoulder. Isaac grabs my hand.

"What's wrong, Nonny?" he frowns.

"I-I fell out with Georgia and Nyah," I sniffle.

It feels *horrible* saying it out loud. It makes it even more real.

"Oh dear. What happened?"

There's no WAY I'm telling her. She'll probably tell me what I already know – that I shouldn't have done what I did.

"It doesn't matter," I sigh, squeezing Isaac's hand.

He smiles up at me and I instantly feel better.

"If it doesn't matter, then you'll be friends again soon, won't you? This isn't the first time this has happened."

She's right: it's not the first time. But it *is* the first time that *I've* caused the problem. And it *is* the first time that I've felt this sad. I nod anyway, not wanting to talk about it anymore. I just want to eat my breakfast, play with Isaac and wrap myself in my duvet all day.

"Everything will be fine. Come on, eat your food," my mum assures me, pointing to the plate in front of me.

Usually, my mum's scrambled eggs make everything better. But today, I'm finding them impossible to chew, what with this dark cloud surrounding me. A terrible thought enters my head. It's so terrible that I drop my knife and fork onto the plate with a CLANG and take a deep, shaky breath.

Who am I going to hang around with on Monday?!

It was bad enough being alone on Friday *afternoon*; how am I going to get through a whole *week* of it?!

I think back to yesterday and how horrendous it was. As soon as Amber and Becky had swanned out of the toilet, I wanted nothing more than to run to my friends and tell them the *awful* news. But I couldn't. Instead, I sat in Science in a daze, looking out the window at the overcast sky and daydreaming of better days. The days when I didn't feel like the third member of The Witches, or the days when I had two best friends who I would never dream of hurting.

I think of all the people I could hang out with at school. Georgia and Nyah have each other, and they're probably even closer now that they share a mutual hatred for me, so it's just me who has to seek out new friends. I *have* always wanted to, but not like this. *Sigh.*

I have three options: I could ask Sarah, Frankie or Chioma.

Sarah and her gang love horses. They gallop around the school field at lunchtime, pretending to escape from the stables and run wild into the sunset. I wouldn't fit in with them AT ALL.

Frankie and her crew are *obsessed* with the famous pop singer, Shane Rock. They sit in the computer room at breaktime, drooling over his pictures and singing along to his music.

Georgia, Nyah and I *hate* his songs, and I don't think I could fake the fandom.

Well… looks like it's Chioma left. Chioma and her friends are so brainy and they *always* listen in class. I guess they could help me improve my grades; my dad would be happy, at least. Maybe they're my best bet.

So, after a restless and lonely weekend with just a three-year-old to talk to, I sidle up to Chioma on Monday. I feel like a peasant begging a queen to have mercy on her. It's mortifying!

"*Heeey,* Chioma!" I croon, grimacing inside.

Chioma looks up at me from the book she's reading and smiles. "Oh, hey, Nonny. What's up?"

Here I go. No going back now.

"I was w-wondering if I could hang out with you this week? I… fell out with Georgia and Nyah," I squeak, feeling my face getting warmer.

"Yeah, sure," she beams, without even hesitating. "You can meet us by the Science block at break."

I breathe a long, grateful sigh of relief. "Thanks so much! See you there," I grin.

Well, that was easier than I thought. WOOHOO, I won't be alone this week! And I say *this week* because I don't intend on being best-friend-less *next* week. I have to get my friends back as soon as possible.

Daniel strolls past, with none other than Becky by his side. He doesn't even see me. *Ugh.* I've been so wrapped up in my best friend drama that I had almost forgotten about this dire turn of events. It's even *more* important that I get my best friends back now, especially if I want to save Daniel from becoming Becky's boyfriend. I'm going to need all the help I can get! But first, I need to get through breaktime.

Gulp.

When the bell rings for breaktime I get a very weird, sick feeling in my tummy. I should be skipping to the canteen to meet Georgia and Nyah and talk about the fantastic sleepover we just had at the weekend. Instead, I'm off to meet clever Chioma and her equally clever friends, who are basically *strangers* to me. What if they don't like me? What if I have nothing in common with any of them? I inhale deeply as I get closer. Chioma has her back to me, and her friends, Cleo and Iesha, are leaning against the decaying Science building, flicking through a magazine.

Cleo's favourite colour is red; I can tell by the scarlet ribbons wrapped around her pigtail buns and the red-rimmed glasses perched on her nose. Even behind her thick lenses I can see she has the longest eyelashes I've ever seen – *without* mascara. She's lucky. *And* she has clear skin! Ugh. WHY did I have to get this bulbous pimple on my chin this morning?

Iesha's eyes are shaped like almonds and her hair is slicked back into a tight ponytail. Her bright pink backpack makes my bedraggled tote bag look even *more* dull. Iesha looks like she hopped straight out of a back-to-school uniform catalogue; her shirt is ironed to PERFECTION! If my mum ever lays eyes on her, she'll definitely wish *she* was her daughter.

I clear my throat and tap Chioma on the shoulder. She turns to greet me.

"Hey, Nonny!" she grins.

Cleo and Iesha look at us, confused. My hand awkwardly travels to my chin to cover my pimple.

"Oh yeah, guys," Chioma says, looking back at her friends. "Nonny's gonna hang out with us this week."

She turns back to me and gives me a warm smile. I already feel so much better. I wave awkwardly at Cleo and Iesha. I can tell they don't want me here, but if I stick with Chioma, everything should be fine.

"Err… hi," Iesha says cautiously.

Cleo doesn't say a word; she just inspects me from head to toe behind her glasses. I feel exposed, as though someone has just burst into the toilet while I'm using it.

Say something, Nonny.

"W-what are you guys reading?" I ask, gripping onto my bag handle so that no one can see my hands shaking.

I don't read celebrity magazines, but if acting interested means that Cleo and Iesha will like me, then I'll do it. Iesha looks down at the magazine then holds it up for me to see. I read the title: *The Truth about Magnetic Fields.*

Oh.

"Uh… *cool,*" I nod, not having a CLUE what it even means.

"Yeah, it is cool," Cleo utters.

I smile at her, but she stares blankly back at me.

"Isn't Miss Hill such a *rubbish* teacher, Nonny?" Chioma asks, peeling the skin off a banana.

I've never thought she was. I mean, I barely listen in Maths anyway; I just stare at Daniel, so maybe she is rubbish. Who knows?

"Erm… I guess," I agree, wanting to have at least *something* to talk about.

"I showed my dad my homework and he says that the stuff she teaches us is for babies. I'm so bored of learning about quadratic expansions and simplification. I want something *more*, you know?" she sighs, chomping on her banana.

I gawk at her, gormless. *WHAT?*

"*Yeaaah,* I know what you mean," I fib.

I don't know how I'm going to keep up this act; I'm already exhausted. I *never* have to pretend to be something I'm not around Georgia and Nyah. They're probably at our usual table right now, giggling at one of Georgia's jokes or gasping at the gossip on Nyah's phone.

"So, how comes you're hanging out with us now?" Iesha asks, rolling up the magazine and tucking it under her arm.

I glance at Chioma, wanting her to answer for me, but her mouth is crammed with the banana she just bit into. I look back at Cleo and Iesha, who are both impatiently awaiting my response.

"Errrrm… me, Georgia and Nyah fell out," I mumble, squirming under their gaze.

"Oh. Why?" Cleo grills, pushing her glasses further up her nose.

"It's a long story," I say, even though it's not.

I messed up our friendship over Daniel because I was jealous. The End.

"Okay," Cleo shrugs.

Phew.

"I'm sure you'll sort it out soon," Chioma assures me.

"Thanks, Chioma."

"So, what are we gonna do at lunch today, guys? Shall we sunbathe?" Chioma asks.

My eyes light up. *Yes!* Finally – something we have in common! I'm about to jump in and yell YES, but *Cleo* gets there first.

"I thought we were gonna go to Science Club today?"

"Ohhh, yeah! Duh! Thanks for reminding me," Chioma giggles.

Science Club?! I feel as deflated as a balloon that's just been viciously popped.

"You don't mind, do you, Nonny?" Chioma asks.

Of COURSE I mind! I don't want to spend a nice, sunny day cooped up in a Science building that stinks of burning plastic and poisonous chemicals. I want to be out on the school field, soaking up the sun and enjoying a fruity ice lolly!

"No, I don't mind at all," I lie, smiling falsely until my cheeks hurt.

"Cool, I can't wait!" Iesha grins. I'm wailing inside, but I keep my mouth shut and my smile on my face.

How am I going to do this?

When I get home, I promise myself that I'm going to make up with my besties TOMORROW. I cannot *bear* another lunchtime with Chioma and her clique, watching them obsess over Bunsen burners and molecules, or nursing the dents in my nose (thanks to those awfully tight Science goggles).

Tomorrow, I'm getting my friends back.

***

"Hey, Georgia," I whisper, sitting beside her in English on Tuesday afternoon.

But Georgia doesn't even flinch.

Gosh, this is going to be HARD! She sits with her body turned slightly away from me while Mrs Sandhu jabbers about how to use semicolons correctly. I slip her a note, trying to tell her all about Becky's recent news.

I'm so so so sorry Georgia!!!

Please forgive me :(

I have something to tell you, something important!!

But as soon as she sees it, she scrunches it up into a ball and pushes it aside like it has lurgies. She doesn't even read it.

That's it. I *need* to do something better. I need to prove how sorry I *truly* am.

After school, while everyone spills out into the corridor and skips into the sun, I stall outside Georgia's Spanish classroom. I peek through the window in the door, preparing myself to enter. Mrs Blackwell's fleshy arm jiggles as she cleans the whiteboard. It's quite warm today, so a strand of her greying hair sticks to her forehead and her upper lip glistens with sweat. I clear my throat, even though I don't need to, and knock lightly.

She looks at me, startled. "Come in!" she calls.

I take a deep breath and do as I'm told. Stepping inside, I exhale shakily. The odour of thirty clammy bodies stuffed inside a small room clings to the air. I feel even more queasy.

"Hi, Miss," I mumble.

"Hello," she replies, watching me strangely. I must look even more nervous than I thought. "Everything okay?"

I start to nod, then quickly stop myself. *Nothing* is okay.

I shake my head instead.

"I've come to apologise for something," I murmur, looking down at my scuffed school shoes.

Mrs Blackwell puts the board rubber on the desk and takes a seat in her tattered chair. "For what?"

I swallow. It's time.

"I did something really bad. My best friend, Georgia… she's in your class. And… well, she had a presentation last week, but I… I ruined it," I admit, ashamed all over again. I wring my hands behind my back. "I was mad at her about something, so I hid her notes and she couldn't remember her lines. It's all my fault, Miss. She didn't deserve bad marks. *Please* can she re-do her presentation? Or… or I can even give you her notes! They're in my room at home. Please?"

I plead. I'm looking at her now, my eyes welling with tears.

Mrs Blackwell tuts softly and slightly shakes her head. "What's your name?"

"Nonny."

"Well, Nonny, thank you for being honest. Although, I'm very disappointed. Have you spoken to Georgia? I'm sure she'd be hurt by your actions."

I nod, wiping the lone tear that's just landed on my cheek. "She hates me. She won't forgive me," I whisper.

Mrs Blackwell sighs deeply. "I'll see what I can do for Georgia. As for you, Nonny, I'm afraid I'll need to request a lunchtime detention for you. What's your form tutor's name?"

My heart sinks. I've NEVER had a detention before! You'll only find the *really* bad students there – the ones who chew gum during lessons, or don't listen to the teachers, or

NEVER do their homework! And I've only ever heard horror stories about what happens in that frightful hall – like Year Eleven's worst offenders terrorising the mouthy Year Sevens, or the boisterous Year Nines gnashing their teeth and attacking the supervisor with balls made out of paper. I shudder at the thought, but I know it's only *half* of what I deserve. Mrs Blackwell peels off a neon-green sticky note and looks at me, awaiting my answer.

"Mr Greaves," I state reluctantly, my voice quavering.

I watch with bated breath as Mrs Blackwell's pudgy fingers grip her pen. She quickly scrawls a note to Mr Greaves, then puts the pen back in her desk drawer.

"I'll give this to him tomorrow morning," she says, patting the note. "But I'm glad you owned up, Nonny. Admitting you did something wrong can be a difficult thing to do."

She's got *that* right.

"Thanks, Miss."

I start walking towards the door, worried sick about tomorrow's detention, but hopeful that Georgia will be able to re-do her presentation and get the top marks she deserves.

"And Nonny?" Mrs Blackwell calls after me.

I turn to face her. "Yes, Miss?"

"I hope you've learnt your lesson."

I nod. "I have."

It's true – I really have. I leave the room and pull my phone from my blazer pocket. With jittery thumbs, I send Georgia a text.

Me: Hey Georgia. I told Mrs Blackwell everything so hopefully you can do your presentation again. I'm really sorry and I hope you can forgive me!!! xxx

After she discarded my secret note in English, I don't expect her to reply (although I really, *really* want her to). I just hope she knows how sorry I am.

Now that I've come clean to Mrs Blackwell, it's time to make it up to Nyah and her parents. I know exactly what I have to do, but I'm *petrified!*

I take my time getting home, wondering if I'm ever going to get my best friends back. I dawdle along the pavement, my brain ticking over, when I catch sight of the most magnificent stone I've EVER seen. I gasp and pick it up, turning it over in my hand. It's burgundy, spattered in white and grey specks that could be mistaken for gold dust. WOW – this could rival my Magic Stone!

"Ewwwwwww!" a shrill voice behind my head screeches.

I nearly jump out of my skin and turn my head to follow the voice.

The Witches.

"You're so *weird!* Why are you picking things up from the *floor?*" Amber taunts.

Ugh – I didn't know they were behind me! I clench my new stone tightly.

"That's what tramps do, Amber. Nonny's a tramp, hahaha!" Becky chortles.

"I'm gonna tell everyone what we just saw you do! Ewww, I can't believe you pick things up from the floor!"

"It's a *stone!*" I insist, shuffling with embarrassment.

The Witches look at each other and snort with laughter.

"*What?* Why are you picking up dirty stones? Ewww, stay away from her, Becky; she's probably got a disease now!" Amber shrieks.

"AAHHH! Stay away from us, Nonny! Nonny has a disease, everyone! Stay away from her!" Becky cries.

Amber scampers away and Becky follows, laughing madly and throwing up a rude gesture with her hand. My blood boils. I so wanted to take my new stone home with me, but I chuck it back to the place I found it, feeling pathetic. My hatred for The Witches, especially *Becky,* has just multiplied. I didn't think it could.

When I get home, I regret abandoning my new stone, so I fetch my Magic Stone instead. I hug it to my chest, desperately hoping for courage, so I can make things right with Nyah.

I need privacy, so I barricade my bedroom door with my chair. *(Sorry, Isaac – I can't be disturbed right now.)* I settle on my bed and place my Magic Stone on my lap for comfort. My hands shake as I search for Nyah's home phone number in my phone. To be honest, I have NO idea what I'm going to say. All I know is that I need to apologise to her parents. So, without hesitation, I press "Call" and hold the phone to my ear.

Ring, ring. Ring, ring. Ring, ring. Ring, ring.

Where is everyone? Someone must be in. Nyah's definitely at home by now, and her mum–

"Hello?" Nyah's mum says, as cheerful and warm as ever.

I stiffen.

"Uh, h-hi aunty. It's… it's Nonny," I gabble, my voice cracking.

"Oh, hello, Nonny! How are you, sweetheart?" She pauses slightly, then says in a hushed tone, "Nyah told me things aren't too great between you girls at the moment."

My heart pumps noisily in my ears, nearly drowning her out. I bite my lip hard. Does she know *everything?*

"Yeah… that's true. And it's all my fault. I… I did something really horrible, aunty, and I want to say sorry."

She sighs. "Yes, Nyah did say. To tell you the truth, Nonny, I was shocked. You're a lovely girl, and you and Nyah are great friends, so it hurt me to hear what had happened. No boy should ever come between such a beautiful friendship. Nyah sees you as a sister – you know that, right?"

Regret sits in my stomach, as heavy and as hefty as a brick.

"I know, and I see her as a sister too!" I cry, grabbing my Magic Stone. "I'm SO sorry! I just… I got so scared that Daniel liked her more than me. That's why I made up those *horrible* lies. I-I don't know what came over me."

"Mhmm. You know… I always tell Nyah that life is too short to stay angry. That's why Nyah's dad and I aren't angry at you, Nonny. And I know for sure that Nyah will forgive you soon. I was young once; I did silly things too. Making mistakes is all a part of growing up. I just hope you've learnt from this."

I nod nonstop, relief coursing through my veins. "I really have. Thank you for forgiving me. I just hope Nyah does too. And I promise I'll *never* say a bad word about you guys again. You're the nicest mum anyone could ever have."

"Oh, Nonny," she laughs heartily. "Don't

worry about me, honey. I've had people say a *lot* worse about me! But you know what? I'm proud of you for being brave enough to call us and apologise. Nyah probably needs some space though, so just respect that for now."

I wish she *didn't* need space because I miss her LOADS. But her mum is right.

"Okay," I sigh. "Can you please tell Nyah I love her?"

"I will do, Nonny. Tell your mum I said hello, won't you?"

"I will."

"Okay, sweetheart. Take care."

She hangs up, and I slump onto my bed, drained. I realise my palms are moist, so I wipe them on my duvet, then close my eyes. I want to text Nyah, but I know I need to follow her mum's advice if she's ever going to forgive me. Plus, I still haven't got a reply from Georgia, so I know Nyah wouldn't respond either.

Ugh. It's been such an exhausting, lonely day. I'm *super* tired, but thoughts still whiz through my mind at lightning speed. I clasp my Magic Stone tight, this time hoping it keeps Becky far, far away from Daniel.

I know what you're thinking – I should have learnt my lesson from all my plots that have gone wrong. But Daniel deserves SO much better than Becky! And he *needs* to know how wretched she is, even if he's not going to be my boyfriend, after all. That's right; I've finally realised that Daniel is NOT going to be my boyfriend. I *finally* understand that my friendship with Georgia and Nyah is one million times more important, and that I would have my best friends back over *him* any day. But that doesn't stop me from wanting to release him from Becky's grip! The only thing is… I can't do it alone. The Witches are *scary*, and together, they pretty much run the whole of

Year Eight, so there's no *way* I could go against Becky by myself.

But I don't have any friends right now.

This week has been one of the worst weeks I've EVER had. I've had to try and survive (just about) without my two BFFs *and* I've had to live with the fact that Becky Ritchcraft is trying to dig her venomous claws into Daniel. Plus, I've had to face The Witches all on my own!

On Wednesday afternoon, after my DREADFUL detention, they block the entrance to my locker. Amber folds her arms across her chest. Her hair is tied up with a snakeskin scrunchie and she's wearing that same strawberry-scented perfume she wore when she crashed my party. *Ugh.* Becky loiters close behind, pouting scornfully. She's knotted the bottom of her school blouse so that it looks like a trendy crop top.

How does she get away with these things?

Every time I step to the side, Amber steps out even faster to stop me from getting past. It's like we're doing some sort of weird, heated dance routine.

"Please move," I snap angrily.

I am NOT in the mood. In detention, a rowdy Year Ten with a smattering of pimples on his forehead had sat behind me, kicking the back of my chair every ten seconds. I had turned around to glare at him, only for him to belch RIGHT in my face. It was *revolting*.

"Don't think you've got away with scratching my face off! I told you my mum's coming for you, remember? So, you better watch out."

"Yes, I *know*," I sigh, rolling my eyes.

"Where are your stupid friends? Not here to back baby Nonny up today, are they?" Amber leers. She hurls Becky a quick look, giving her the go-ahead to speak.

I shrug, looking down.

"HA! Have they *finally* ditched you?" Becky teases.

That hurts like a kick to the stomach.

"Leave me alone," I mumble.

"Leave me alone," Amber mimics cruelly. "Looks like they finally got tired of all your *crying*. Waaah, waahhh, I'm Nonny, all I do is CRY!"

Don't cry, don't cry, don't cry!

"No, I DON'T! Now get out of my way," I seethe.

"Do your friends know you're a *tramp* who likes to pick up things from the floor?" she jeers.

"I'm gonna tell Mrs Sullivan if you don't move," I say.

"Ooooh," Amber scoffs, shaking her hands in front of her to pretend she's scared. "Becky, did you hear that? Nonny's gonna get the headteacher on us like a *baby*. See if *we* care. Anyway, just you wait, loser. We're coming for you."

And with that, they're gone.

I stick my head into my locker, trying to hold back my tears. I'm even more vulnerable against The Witches without my best friends by my side. Even though all of us are pretty useless when it comes to standing up to them, it always helped to know that we had each other's backs. And now, with one of The Witches trying to cast a love spell on Daniel, I need my friends more than ever.

I don't know what's worse; fighting with Georgia and Nyah, or watching helplessly as Becky and Daniel get closer every day. She's been clinging onto him like a baby to a blanket. It's *sickening*. I saw them together *again* earlier,

Becky throwing her head back with laughter at Daniel's jokes, and Daniel hanging onto Becky's every toxic word. I'd be lying if I said it didn't hurt, and that I didn't wish Becky would just hop on her broomstick and disappear FOREVER, but all I *really* care about right now is getting my best friends back.

I'm grateful to have had Chioma and her friends, but let's face it – they're not Georgia and Nyah. I feel like an outsider when they crack up at their inside jokes, and like a four-year-old when they share their smarty-pants riddles that I don't understand in the slightest. So, I decide that I'll brave school on my own from now on. The library has become my new safe haven for the rest of the week. It's the only place I can go where I know I won't bump into Georgia and Nyah *or* The Witches.

It's crazy how much my life has changed. Just last week, my besties and I were a tremendous trio. Now, I avoid our spot by the potted plants when I arrive at school and I linger in my classrooms longer than I should, so I don't see either of them. I miss my best friends. I miss us sitting at lunch together and laughing until our stomachs cramp and our jaws ache. I miss Georgia and Nyah quibbling over stupid things, like when Nyah couldn't stop laughing at Georgia's poor attempt at painting her nails, or when Nyah finished the last sweet without asking Georgia if she wanted it first.

I wish I had never done what I did.

***

I'm late for History on Friday morning – on purpose, of course. I meander through the corridor, picturing being in the park with my besties, pushing Georgia on the swing and

Nyah recording all the fun on her phone.

Someone emerges from the toilet ahead of me, pausing my daydream. I squint. I'd recognise those long, neat braids anywhere.

"Nyah!" I call, loud enough for her to hear, but quiet enough to not get scalded by any hot-headed teachers. She turns and rolls her eyes when she sees it's me.

"Nyah, please talk to me," I plead, scuttling after her like a lost puppy. I know her mum told me to give her space, but I'm *desperate* for her to speak to me.

"What do you want, Nonny?" she sighs, folding her arms.

"I want you back as my best friend. You and Georgia. And I want to say sorry. I really, really mean it," I pant, out of breath from chasing her down the corridor.

"It's too late for that," she says bluntly.

My heart sinks.

"So… you never want to be my friend again?"

Nyah looks away.

"Nyah?"

"We just don't want to talk to you right now, Nonny. You really upset us. And I know you spoke to my mum, but that doesn't mean I'll forgive you straightaway."

"I know. I just wanted to apologise to your parents because I felt terrible. I *wish* you could feel how sorry I am. I miss you guys so much," I wail.

Nyah doesn't say anything. I know she misses me too, but I *also* know she won't back down.

"Anyway, I have something to tell you– " I start, ready to tell her all about Becky.

"GIRLS! Get to your lessons, now," Mrs Grant yaps, sticking her head out of her classroom door.

Nyah immediately strides off without saying a word. I glare at Mrs Grant. I was so close! What am I supposed to do now? Georgia *still* won't accept my notes in English and she *still* sits turned away from me like I have some sort of infectious disease. And Nyah can't even bear to say more than two words to me.

Will I *ever* get my friends back?

Tonight is yet another boring Friday night. My horrific lunchtime detention was probably the highlight of my week. I sit huddled up in bed, avoiding my family while they all watch something about the animal kingdom downstairs. It's been a whole *week* without my best friends. It feels like I've gone a whole week without my arms or legs. It's been so difficult, but I'm *determined* to get them back – TONIGHT! Not only do I need their help keeping Daniel away from Becky, but all I want is for us to go back to normal, just like how we were *before* I messed everything up. I've decided I'm going to send them a text. They could easily ignore me, but if I try and catch their attention straightaway, maybe that'll work!

I sit cross-legged in my bed and nervously send a message to our group chat (which they haven't kicked me out of, luckily).

Me: Becky likes Daniel!!!!!!! I heard her talking in the toilet, I've been trying to tell u all week!! I know u hate me so much and I'm so so sorry. I can't say it enough! Pls forgive me and let's save Daniel from Becky together. <3 u guys xxx

I wait. And wait. *And wait.*

After what feels like an entire day has passed, I hear a loud BZZZZ. I've got a message! My heartbeat speeds up as I pick up my phone.

IT'S FROM NYAH!

Nyah: What????

She's shocked, which is great! It means she cares. Another BZZZZ – this time from Georgia!

Georgia: EWWW!! Why does she like him??? I hope he doesn't like her back!

I jump out of bed, so excited. My besties are finally replying to me! *And* they're both as surprised as I thought they would be!

Me: I know right!!! She said she's going to make him her boyfriend! We can't let this happen!!!

I await the rapid replies from my besties, expressing their disgust and horror.

But a minute passes. Then two. I watch my phone screen as obsessively as my favourite TV show. My friends are taking awfully long to reply all of a sudden. What's going on?

Then… BZZZZ!

Nyah: Do u only want us to help u cos u want him to yourself?

I shake my head in disbelief. This is how my besties see me now – and it's all my fault. This is bad. I sit back down on my bed, feeling a familiar, bulky weight on my shoulders.

Me: Of course not, I promise! I know he's not going to be my boyfriend and I don't want him to be anymore, especially after what I did to u guys :(I just don't want him to be with Becky because she's so horrible!!!

Nyah: Hmmmm okay

Georgia: So what do u wanna do?

What *do* I want to do? What will keep Daniel away from Becky forever? I think long and hard, my thumbs hovering above my phone screen.

I've got it.

Me: I've got a plan, don't worry :)

Nyah: WOOHOO! I can't wait to get her back for all the bad things she's done to us!

Georgia: Same! What's the plan Nonny?

Me: I'll tell you at school on Monday! Thanks guys I can't wait :D

Nyah: This doesn't mean I forgive u by the way

Georgia: Same

That's good enough for me! My heart leaps with joy and I prance around my room with my hands in the air. Even though my besties *said* they don't forgive me, I still hope they have. Regardless, I get to hang out with them again on Monday! I can finally wave goodbye to the musty library and its dusty books, and I'll NEVER have to set foot in another Science Club again! And it's all because of Becky – one half of the nastiest duo at school – that my besties and I are back together. I should thank her.

Plus, I've finally hatched a fantastic plan that:

1. Won't upset my best friends; and

2. Might just work!

I don't know if I'll ever get over the fact that Daniel doesn't like me in the way I like *him* (even if I *did* wreck my friendship with my two bestest friends to try and get closer to him). But one thing's for sure. We've GOT to put a stop to this romance between him and Witch #2.

And I know how.

We meet in the computer room at lunchtime on Monday, looking around shiftily for anyone who might clock what we're up to. It's like we're on a top-secret mission for the FBI, like we're *spies* or something. It's great!

Nyah grabs a piece of paper from the printer and scurries back to us, looking very pleased with herself. But when she picks up her pen to start writing, she frowns. Georgia and I glance at each other, confused.

"What are you doing?" Georgia asks.

"Yeah, we need to hurry up," I urge, checking the time. "Come on, write something!"

"I-I don't know what to write!"

"Just write the meanest things that come to your head," Georgia insists, pushing Nyah's hand so that the pen grazes the paper.

Nyah hesitates. "Are you sure? I'd feel so bad writing mean things about you."

"But they're meant to be from *Becky*, remember, not from you! Just write all the things you've ever heard her say to me."

I should probably tell you what's going on, right? Well… we're going to set Becky up! EEEEK – it was all my idea and I'm so proud of it. We're going to forge a horrible note from Becky, plant it in Georgia's bag, then she's going to open it in front of Daniel so he can see how EVIL Becky really is! Georgia has Spanish with him last period, so she's going to sit next to him again (she moved to another seat following her humiliating Spanish presentation, but she's moving back JUST for this plan!). She loves Drama and she's *sooo* good at playing different characters, so I know she'll even be able to *cry* on cue! Daniel will be so horrified by Becky's cruel words that he'll never talk to her again. It's PERFECT!

But now, Nyah is biting her lip and rubbing her forehead as though she's in pain. She holds the pen just above the piece of paper, wondering what to write.

"Oh, for goodness' sake! I'll do it," Georgia sighs, grabbing the pen.

"Wait!" I cry, before she begins. "Doesn't Daniel know what your handwriting looks like?"

Georgia pauses and claps her hands to her cheeks. "Oh my gosh. He does!" she exclaims, worried.

I groan.

"Don't panic! Just change your writing a bit. Easy!" Nyah jumps in, saving the day.

"Yes!" I cheer, perking up. "Great idea, Nyah!"

Georgia nods slowly, then grins mischievously. "Okay."

Pressing her lips tightly together, she starts to write in big, loopy letters – *nothing* like her usual writing. Nyah and I watch in amazement as the pen bobs along the paper; we didn't know she had this trick up her sleeve! We're also surprised that she's happily reliving all the horrible things Becky has said to her. But we all know it'll be worth it when Daniel finally sees Becky's true colours.

You're a HUGE loser and you should ~~exere~~ exercise and stop stuffing ur face with junk food cos you are HUGE!!!

And your friends are losers too you're all loserrrrrrssss. And no one likes you!!! From Becky

Georgia sits back and admires her handiwork.

"*Wooooow,*" Nyah breathes. "That's literally something Becky would say!"

"Yeah, it is!" I agree, giggling.

Okay, so, maybe Georgia's "new" handwriting isn't the *best* disguise, but let's just hope Daniel is none the wiser. All we need him to focus on is what *Becky* has written.

I'm extra happy today. I've finally got my best friends back and we're about to bring Becky DOWN! Being with my besties again feels like snuggling into my warm, cosy bed after a long, miserable day in the rain. It *was* a little awkward at breaktime, since it was the first time that I'd sat with them in just over a week. I had to wipe the sweat from my forehead and take a sip of water to calm my nerves before I sat down. Georgia and Nyah eyed me suspiciously.

"Hey, guys," I mumbled.

"Hi."

"Hey."

I gulped and cleared my throat, ready to recite the mini-speech I'd been practising all morning in the mirror. "I've really missed you guys. A-and I'm really sorry. I… I never wanted to hurt you, and I promise I'll never, ever, ever do ANYTHING like that again!"

I sat with my hands in my lap, checking my besties' faces for any sign of forgiveness.

Eventually, Georgia sighed and shrugged. "It's fine. I'm over it now, anyway. Plus, Mrs

Blackwell said I can do my presentation again. Let's just forget about it."

I grinned so hard I could barely see. We both turned to Nyah to see what she thought. I held my breath nervously, hoping she'd feel the same.

"Same," she shrugged. "And... we missed you too. We just wish you would have told us how much you really liked Daniel, then none of this would have happened."

I nodded along ecstatically. If I was a puppy, I would have been wagging my tail.

"I know, I know. I wish I would have done too. I guess I was just embarrassed to tell you how much I liked him," I admitted. "I didn't want you to think I was crazy, even though I ended up being... quite crazy."

Georgia and Nyah sniggered.

"Yeah, you're actually a *lunatic*. I was only teasing you when I used to call you crazy; I didn't actually *mean* it! But now I'm never going to like anyone you like – EVER again!" Georgia laughed.

"Same! I would fear for my LIFE!" Nyah joked.

They both doubled over in stitches, clutching their stomachs. It's not the greatest feeling to be laughed at by your two BFFs in the world, but I guess I deserved it. I eventually joined in with them, just happy to be back with them.

"Let's never keep secrets from each other ever again," Nyah said, once the laughter had died down.

"Yeah, and let's NEVER let a boy get in between us again, either," Georgia added.

"Definitely. Let's stick together forever," I beamed.

Then, we performed our special three-way handshake without ANY mistakes. And that's when I knew everything would be okay again.

Georgia neatly folds the piece of paper and places it in her bag, ready for our big plan to begin.

"Eeeek, I hope this works!" she squeals.

All we need to do now is get through afternoon form time, then we can put Operation Take Becky Down into action! Georgia will call us after school to let us know how it went. I can't WAIT!!!

Instead of listening in Religious Studies, I picture Georgia innocently unfolding the note and dramatically gasping in shock to get Daniel's attention. He'll turn to her, curious to know what's going on, then Georgia will start crying and show him the note. Daniel will be so appalled by Becky's spitefulness that he'll never talk to her again, and me and my besties would have successfully completed our mission! I grin to myself and turn the page of my textbook to catch up with the rest of the class.

***

It's five o'clock. I've been expecting Georgia's call since four, so I've been worried sick! I even sent a message to our group chat to find out where she is.

Me: Where are u Georgia? Hurry up and let us know what happened!

Nyah: Yeah where are u Georgia!! We need to know if it worked!

At about half past five, she finally messages us back.

Georgia: Sorry guys I was in after school detention. I'll call u now to explain

After-school detention?!

If I thought lunchtime detention was bad, after-school detention is TEN times worse. Georgia might be loud, but what could she have possibly done to get an after-school detention?

I answer the phone as soon as it rings. "Why did you get an after-school detention?" I blurt immediately.

"Yeah, what did you *do?*" Nyah chuckles. "It must have been pretty bad!"

"It's WORSE than bad!" Georgia moans.

Oh no.

"What happened? Is it something to do with our plan?" I gulp, knowing that it is.

"Yep," Georgia sighs. "I did everything we said. I got out the note and I gasped really loud. But… I think it was *too* loud."

"What do you *mean?*" Nyah interrupts, annoyed.

"Well, *everyone* turned to look at me, not just Daniel!" Georgia whines. "So then, Mrs Blackwell screamed at me for disrupting the class, and she came over and snatched the note from me!"

"Noooooo!" I wail. "So Daniel didn't get to see it at all?"

"No, he didn't. And horrible Mrs Blackwell ripped it up in front of *everyone* and gave me detention for disrupting the class!" Georgia exclaims. "I hate her! She ruined the plan!"

"You shouldn't have made such a loud noise, Georgia! This wouldn't have happened otherwise!" Nyah flares.

"Why are you blaming *me?* Mrs Blackwell was the one who ripped the note up! I could've got it back at the end of the lesson if she wasn't so angry!"

"It's not your fault, Georgia," I say. We don't have time for an argument right now, so I need to make sure we get back on track. "We just need to think of another plan, that's all."

"But this plan was perfect! This SUCKS!" Nyah cries. "What are we gonna do *now?*"

"Hmmm... we could give *Daniel* a fake note instead?" Georgia suggests.

"No WAY! If he's close with Becky, he can just ask her why she wrote it and he'll soon find out that she didn't!" Nyah reminds us.

"That's true. That probably wouldn't work," I sigh.

There's a silence on the line as we all rack our brains for another plan. I'm upset that our first one didn't work, but there's no time to sulk about it. We have to act quickly.

"I've got it!" Georgia proclaims. "I know what we can do, guys!"

"What?" Nyah and I reply, excited.

"The Witches have to pass your locker to get to *their* lockers, right, Nonny?"

"Yeah..."

"Well, before lunch tomorrow, you and Nyah should meet at your locker. The Witches will walk past, so one of you can say something to annoy them – *especially* Becky. Then, they'll start being really mean, right? Daniel and I have Spanish before lunch, so I'll make sure he comes with me to meet you guys. Then, we'll walk in on The Witches being extra horrible, and Daniel will be able to see Becky for who she really is!" Georgia burbles, without taking a breath.

The information whirls around my brain like a tornado. And when it finally settles, I realise something. Georgia's plan is... PERFECT!

"EEEEK, I love it!" I screech, punching the air in victory.

"Me too. It's such a good idea!" Nyah agrees.

Once we've sorted out how the plan is going to work, we hang up, buzzing with excitement. We're *finally* going to get Becky, and we're going to get her good!

I'm a nervous wreck when the bell rings for lunch on Tuesday afternoon. We both are. Nyah's hands tremble, and sweat trickles from my forehead as we stand awkwardly by my locker, waiting for The Witches to strut by.

"Nonny... should we really do this?" Nyah whispers. She cracks her knuckles nervously and takes a deep breath.

I want to say NO and run far, far away. I'm *petrified,* wondering what will happen to us when we go after The Witches.

Why did we agree to this again?

"We have to," I whisper back. "We just have to be brave."

But I don't feel brave at all. I'm a scaredy-cat, terrified of what The Witches will say and do to us. But I don't have time to give in to the fear, because… here they come! Amber's long, blonde hair sways behind her as she swaggers towards us. Becky's hair is in a bun on the top of her head and her school skirt is rolled up at the waist so it's even shorter than usual.

"*Look* who it is, Becky! Trampy Nonny and loser Nyah," Amber hollers, stopping in front of me. Becky does the same to Nyah, blocking her potential escape route.

Gulp.

"Yeah, well, you're… you're..." Nyah stumbles, messing up the line we rehearsed over and over again at breaktime. She desperately nudges me for help.

"You're a nasty person with no friends. *Becky* doesn't even like you," I garble in record time.

I only talk this fast when I'm nervous. And I sure am nervous.

"*What* did you say?" Becky erupts, pushing her way past Amber and Nyah to get close to me. Her nose nearly skims mine.

I step back, but she follows me like my shadow.

"You heard what she said. You only hang out with Amber because you're scared of her," Nyah murmurs.

I secretly squeeze her hand. We're doing it. We're actually doing it!

"You better shut up RIGHT now, Nyah. The only person who's scared right now is YOU! You look like you're about to pee your pants, just like last time. HA! Do you and Nonny *both* wear nappies?" Amber jumps in.

Becky cackles. "Nonny's just getting brave

because you haven't got her back for attacking you, Amber. But I think you should get her back RIGHT NOW!"

I flinch, scared stiff.

Come ON Georgia; where are you?!

"If you do that, we're going straight to Mrs Sullivan. So, don't you dare!" Nyah squeaks.

"As if I'm scared of Mrs *Sullivan*. We're not scared of that wrinkly old lady. Are we, Becky?" Amber spits, knocking my shoulder so that I stagger backwards.

Oh my gosh, she's going to hit me! *Where are Georgia and Daniel?!*

"No way! We told you that you were gonna pay for what you did to Amber. And *you* can get a black eye too, *Nyah,*" Becky hisses, pushing Nyah's forehead with her index finger.

"Don't touch me," Nyah growls.

"Yeah, you don't have to do everything your *boss* does, Becky," I smirk, trying really hard to push her buttons.

Adrenaline rushes through me; it feels GREAT to tell The Witches what we really think of them. All we need now is for Georgia and Daniel to come round the corner and catch her out. Where *are* they?

"She's *not* the boss of me, you little–" Becky starts, until something in the distance catches her eye. Or should I say… *someone?*

Nyah and I swing around to see Georgia and Daniel approaching us. FINALLY!!! I'm so relieved. I fold my arms defiantly, waiting for Becky to finish her sentence. But she doesn't. Instead, she lightly kicks Amber. Nyah and I steal a puzzled glance. *Why are they not saying anything?* Nyah taps my elbow, urging me to rile Becky up even more.

I clear my throat. "Y-you look silly with that… p-push-up bra," I stutter, waiting for her wrath to pelt down on me like hailstones.

But she doesn't even look at me. In fact, she doesn't say a word.

No!!! No, no, no!

Our plan is failing. It's FAILING!

Daniel and Georgia finally reach us. Georgia is red-faced and flustered. She looks at me and Nyah with an apologetic expression on her face.

"Oh, hey guys!" Daniel grins.

"*Heeeey,* Danny!" Becky smiles sweetly.

Danny? UGH!!!

"I didn't know you guys were friends," Daniel continues, looking around at all of us.

I nearly gag. "We're NOT–" I begin, but Becky's loud voice drowns me out.

"We were just coming to find you. Let's go have lunch," she croons, linking Daniel's arm.

Georgia, Nyah and I watch helplessly as Daniel lets Becky drag him away. Amber gives us a smug look and marches off beside them. My besties and I stand by my locker, our blood boiling and our jaws on the floor. I feel so stupid.

Amber turns back to us and shoots us an evil smile.

"We're coming for you," she mouths silently as she walks away.

I swallow hard. As soon as they're out of sight, Nyah swivels angrily to face Georgia.

"Where *were* you, for goodness' sake? We nearly got beaten up! And you missed everything!"

"I'm *sorry!* Daniel had to ask Mrs Blackwell a question after the lesson and she went on and on and ON! It's not my fault!" Georgia protests.

"Just like *yesterday* wasn't your fault, either?" Nyah snaps, rolling her eyes.

"Nyah, stop. It was *Becky's* fault – she saw Daniel coming!" I sigh, exhausted. "Maybe the plan just wasn't meant to work."

"Of *course* it was meant to work! It just got ruined. Again," Nyah replies, staring pointedly at Georgia.

Georgia looks down, shuffling her feet anxiously. "I really tried to get him to hurry up, you know. But Mrs Blackwell shouted at me *again*. I'm really starting to hate her!"

"Let's just not carry out another plan in your Spanish class," I shrug.

"Let's just not carry out another plan at *all*," Nyah mutters.

I gawp at her, gobsmacked. "*What?* We *have* to!"

I pivot to Georgia for support. But she shrugs guiltily.

"Is there much point? It's obvious that *Danny* likes Becky. There's nothing we can do. Plus, nothing we're doing is working anyway."

I can't BELIEVE it! After all the effort we've put into saving Daniel from Becky, my friends want to throw in the towel!

"Please, guys," I moan, as we start making our way to the canteen. All this drama has made me extremely hungry. "Let's try one more time, at least."

Georgia sighs. "It's too stressful, Nonny. And we've tried already. The Witches always get what they want, and this is no different."

"Yeah, I'm worn out. Sorry, Nonny. Let's just leave it."

Frustrated tears spill from my eyes, but I wipe them away before my besties can see.

"Fine," I mumble. "Let's leave it."

Georgia and Nyah chatter politely with the dinner lady while she serves our lunch, but I don't have the energy to join them. I lumber behind them to our usual spot, and slump into my seat with a loud sigh.

I'm not ready to quit just yet, but I can't keep Daniel away from Becky without the help of my BFFs. It pains me that we're giving up and just letting Becky get whatever she wants, but if Daniel really *does* like her, I guess my friends are right. There really is nothing we can do. *Ugh.*

Now, I just need to worry about The Witches picking up where they left off. I'll need to look over my shoulder every day; they could come back for me at any time! Becky was *fuming*. I shudder at the thought. Still, I'm proud of myself and Nyah for standing up to a bully, even if it *was* part of a plan that failed miserably.

I sink my spoon into my sloppy shepherd's pie and try to forget about what just happened.

Daniel has well and truly fallen for Becky's sickly-sweet act.

The day after Operation Take Becky Down crumbled to pieces before my very eyes, I'm haunted by visions of Witch #2 and Daniel *everywhere* I go. Cuddling in the canteen one minute, frolicking in the foyer the next.

Ugh, I can't take it!

Every time I see the two of them together, I can feel my face contort with envy. If anyone could see me, they'd probably think I had just sucked on the world's most sour lemon.

Once upon a time, Daniel was *Dreamy* Daniel, a galaxy of twinkling stars and magical rainbows in my mind. I'd fall asleep to thoughts of him like my favourite bedtime story. But now? He's a NIGHTMARE. Just like his *girlfriend*.

I don't even know if they're a couple, and I guess I shouldn't care. I have to move on.

I've got Maths now. Usually, Maths is the best part of my day because of *you-know-who,* but the butterflies in my stomach are pretty still today. I'm surprised – confused, even. What does this mean? I walk into the classroom, and out of habit, glance at Daniel's desk out of the corner of my eye. He's not there. I wait for that familiar pang of disappointment and sadness.

But… nothing.

Hmmm. I guess this is… *good,* right?

"Nonny!" Daniel hisses from behind me, making me jump.

I turn to see him outside the Maths classroom with a huge smile on his face. He looks like he's up to something. Then, I see Becky behind him, wearing a mean, glossy pout. Ugh – he's *definitely* up to something. He beckons me over with a wave of his hand, and

I stupidly walk towards him.

"Yeah?" I ask suspiciously.

"Can you do me a huge favour please, Nonny?" he grins, flashing his braces at me.

Where is that special twinge in my heart that I usually feel when he smiles at me like this? *What's going on?*

"What?" I sigh, suddenly irritated.

I glare at Becky over his shoulder, who's mouthing foul words at me. I can't *stand* her.

"I'm gonna bunk Maths today," he whispers dramatically.

I lean back to inspect his face for any sign of a joke. I'm shocked. I thought Daniel was just as much a goody-two-shoes as Chioma!

"Why?"

"I'm gonna go hang out with Becky. Don't tell Miss Hill," he chuckles.

I look at Becky, feeling nauseous. She's corrupting him! He *never* would have done this before he started speaking to her!

Regardless of my outrage, I force a wobbly smile. "So, what's the favour?"

"Well… I was wondering…" he starts, shyly. "Since I'm not gonna be in the lesson, could you write up the notes for me? I'll give you my book."

I eyeball him, barely blinking.

It's official.

I don't like Daniel in the same way I used to. Just a couple of weeks ago, I would have *jumped* at the chance to do this favour for him. I even would have believed that he'd like me more because of it. And I would have been so excited that he'd entrusted me to do it for him! But not anymore.

I take a deep breath and say, "Sorry, Daniel. I don't think I'll be able to."

Wow, I can't *believe* I just did that! I've *never* said no to Daniel before. What I've just done might mean that the special bond we built in our Maths lessons is now broken. But… maybe we never really had a bond to begin with.

"Ah, really? *Please?*" he pleads, batting his eyelashes and clasping his hands together as though he's saying a prayer.

"I–" I start, feeling guilty.

Poor Daniel. I don't want him to think I'm horrible for refusing to help him. If I don't do this favour, he won't be able to catch up in time for our next lesson. Then, Miss Hill will probably embarrass him in front of the whole class like she did to me.

But no. I can't think like that. It's *his* choice to bunk off with *Becky*, not mine! I quickly wrestle with my thoughts, very nearly giving in, but something inside me tells me to stand my ground.

"Sorry. I won't be able to concentrate on my own work if I do that," I state, more confident this time. My dad would be proud.

Daniel sighs, frowning. "It's fine… I understand. I'll ask Nathan instead."

I exhale and nod. "Okay."

"Come *on*, Danny!" Becky calls, chewing on her piece of gum rather loudly.

I scowl at Witch #2 while Daniel looks back at her.

"I'm coming, Bex!" he replies.

Vomit.

He turns back to me, suddenly in a rush. "Thanks anyway, Nonny," he smiles.

I smile back feebly and turn away before I change my mind. It's not until I get to my seat that I realise I've been sweating like crazy. Wow, I really *was* nervous. But I did it! I said no to Daniel for the FIRST TIME EVER! I'm *so* proud of myself.

I feel great, but that doesn't stop me from staring at Daniel's empty seat and wondering what he could *possibly* see in Becky. Maybe he can't see her true colours because he's blinded by her extra-shiny lip gloss. Maybe he's so distracted by her super obvious push-up bra that he can't see her for who she really is. Or… maybe he's just more like her than I thought. If Daniel – sweet, kind, funny Daniel – can like one half of *The Witches,* a gruesome bully with a poisonous personality, then he can't be *that* great. They're *welcome* to each other!

Because I liked him so much, I wasted a lot of time thinking that I had nothing to offer in comparison to my besties. I even went to crazy lengths to ruin their relationships with him because I thought they had more of a chance than *I* did. But it turns out that Daniel never liked any of us anyway – he's clearly always liked *Becky!* Plus, he used *all* of us! He made Georgia prepare the WHOLE Spanish presentation, asked Nyah to return his books to the library and… don't even get me *started* on my Maths homework. My jealousy got me nowhere. And comparing myself to my best friends got me NOWHERE!

So *what* if I have a stone collection hidden away in my room and locker, or I'm not well-known on social media (apart from that time those videos from my birthday party went viral – *cringe*), or I cry more than everyone in the whole world put together? All that means is that I'm unique and sensitive, special and caring. That's what makes me who I am. And my best friends LOVE me for who I am. My little brother, Isaac, loves me, and I guess my parents do, too. That's all that matters.

All I want to do now is stay *well* away from The Witches, plan fun adventures for the summer with my BFFs and forget *all* about silly boys. NOTHING is going to take me away from my friends again – I'll make sure of it! Who wants a *boyfriend*, anyway?

Though I must admit, Josh Harries is quite cute…

Printed in Great Britain
by Amazon